The Warrior with Alzheimer's

The Battle for Justice

A Novel

By

Stephen Woodfin

Produced by Gallivant Press, an imprint of VentureGalleries.com
Venture Galleries
1220 Chateau Lane, Hideaway, Texas 75771.
Phone: 214.564.1493

ISBN: 978-1-937569-69-3

Text: Stephen Woodfin
Editing & Design: Linda Greer Pirtle
Cover Design: Jutta Medina

First Edition

This book is dedicated to the women and men of the Greatest Generation, many of whom now fight their final heroic battle against Alzheimer's disease.

Love's not Time's fool, though rosy lips and cheeks
Within his bending sickle's compass come:
Love alters not with his brief hours and weeks,
But bears it out even to the edge of doom.

»William Shakespeare, "Sonnet 116"

Prologue

THE THING THAT frightened Woody Wilson the most was that he knew he had begun to forget things, not things that didn't matter, like the three way light bulbs on the grocery list, or the hand signals he flashed fifty years before to a little league batter from his coaching spot at third base that meant he should lay down a bunt on the next pitch, or the color of the dress the real estate lady wore when she showed the condo to Maggie and him, or things he liked to forget, like the preacher's sermon from last Sunday, or the dirty joke Carruthers told at the coffee shop the week before, or the gas mileage he once calculated on his old Ford truck, not the things that people attributed to the normal forgetfulness of an old man whose brain had no more room for trivia or whose soul was worn out from five years of killing his fellow man with an M1 rifle in ancient woods where thorns of barbed wire tore his khaki uniform and rivers ran sharp around turns that accelerated the current so that it tumbled bodies over submerged rocks and rendered the human remains in the gurgling water carrion for birds already surfeited; but rather the things that mattered, like the lump he felt in his throat when his baby boy Waylon breathed the first time after the doctor slapped him on the butt, or the dark purple of wispy clouds that framed the brilliant orb of the sun as it sank below the Gulf horizon in late July after a sudden storm, or the last birthday present he had given Maggie, or what he liked about rising early in the morning when it was still dark when he inspected the house to ensure that everyone under his care was safe and accounted for, or why he loved Maggie so desperately, or why he drew his next breath, or spoke kindly to his neighbors, or why he carried a wooden stick clenched in his left hand when he took a walk along the path next to the beach road.

And when he knew he had forgotten those precious things and when he knew he had forgotten other things more precious yet, he didn't go to his friends and ask them to remind him, to reconstitute the cords that held his spirit, to re-invent his character. He sought no re-affirmation of his reputation, no gentle nudge back towards compassion, no hortatory elegy about the ways of the world, no recitation of Shakespeare's stages of man, no biblical reference to the appointed time.

No.

Not Woody Wilson.

When Woody knew he had forgotten, he ran. He ran not towards some distant light, not into the arms of those who still knew who they were and what they thought, but in the direction of the deepest darkness, through the flap that hung open where reality's seam had sagged, into the unknown of the unknowing.

And so it was that at six o'clock on a Saturday morning, when the leaves had just begun to change and the oppressive heat of summer had turned to a cool north breeze, Woody Wilson stuffed everything he owned into his duffle bag and walked down the stairs of his son's home to the front door, stepped outside, took a deep breath and stole his own truck from the driveway.

In the quiet Bowling Green neighborhood other early risers waved in his direction when they heard him start his '64 Ford and coast backwards down the drive. But they didn't look up as they picked weeds from their flower beds and dreamed of the day when they would escape to Florida beach houses and the anonymity of affluence that lay just beyond their reach.

Chapter 1

WHEN WOODY WILSON turned his Ford F150 down the off ramp on I-65 North onto Mohammed Ali Boulevard just south of the Ohio River Bridge in Louisville, Kentucky, he was on the run, confused, but not yet worried, lost, but not yet trapped.

The ramp curled its way to a stop sign where it intersected a one-way street in front of Jewish Hospital.

"We showed that god dammed Adolph Hitler a thing or two," he said as he remembered the horror of the camp he had marched into as nineteen-year-old boy, his rifle slung over his shoulder, his eyes filled with tears, his head hung in shame. He hadn't been able to talk to Maggie about that day for almost ten years after the war.

When he thought about Maggie he remembered their trip to Louisville, her teacher's conference for special needs kids where she was the star presenter and he the tag-a-long postal worker who walked the halls of the Galt House Hotel where he chit-chatted with the other stray husbands.

They had eaten supper at a restaurant on the twenty-fifth floor of the hotel that made a full revolution every forty minutes. From their high vantage point they watched the sunset on the Ohio River. While they held hands, Woody told her things she already knew about the historic river.

"Maggie, if you look over there you can see the Falls of the Ohio," he said as he pointed towards the north shore of the river west of where they sat. "A lot of people drowned trying to get their cargo past those falls."

Maggie looked at him like a school girl hearing all the historical trivia for the first time. She squeezed his hand tightly as he spoke, looked where he pointed, moved her chair a little closer to him as the sun dipped below the horizon.

"Maybe we need to bring the boat up here and take a cruise down the river some time," she said when he finished.

"Let's do it," Woody said. "The *Miss Maggie* would be up to the task."

"She sure would," Maggie said.

Woody made his way west on the boulevard until he hit a red light.

"You can always go right on red," he said as he turned north towards the river.

He drove until a concrete barrier blocked him from driving into the water. He parked his car as close as he could to the river, got out of the truck and walked to the shore.

ALONG THE PIER he found two boats for hire. One was just boarding, so he walked up the gangplank on the *Belle of Louisville* where he met a college kid taking tickets.

"I need to see your ticket, sir," the boy said.

"I'm afraid I don't have one, son," Woody said.

"Do you have eight dollars on you?" the boy asked.

Woody felt around in his pockets and pulled a ten-dollar bill out of the back left.

"That's good enough for me. Enjoy your trip," the ticket taker said as he motioned Woody aboard the vessel.

Woody walked to the rail on the starboard side of the boat, a three-decker facsimile of an old paddle steamer, and held on as he watched the gangplank rise.

The autumn coolness had given way to the last vestiges of summer and all of a sudden he felt hot; his knees began to tremble. He held tight to the rail as he made his way towards the nearest door that opened into the cabin on the first level.

When he entered the cabin, he felt an air-conditioned breeze. To his left was a woman in her early fifties who welcomed him as she pattered on about the history of the river to the other cruisers.

"Take any seat you want, sir," she told him as he walked next to her.

"Have you seen Maggie?" he asked her.

"Maggie who?"

"My wife, the pretty lady who got on with me," Woody said. He had a look on his face like a five-year-old kid separated from his mother at a Halloween carnival. The skin around his eyes sagged into dark bags; his hands, splotched with age spots, trembled like those of a man on the third day of DTs; he shuffled his feet like a prisoner in leg irons.

The tour lady recognized the look, the look her mother used to give her after she progressed far enough into Alzheimer's disease that she could no longer mask it.

"No, sir. I haven't seen her, but I'll look for her right now. What's her name again?"

"Maggie Wilson," Woody said.

"And what's your name, sir?"

Woody looked at her perplexed. He started to give her a piece of his mind but held back. "Woodrow Wilson," he said. "But I go by Woody."

"I'll see if I can find Maggie for you, Mr. Wilson," she said. "In the meantime, why don't you have a seat and enjoy the cruise on the beautiful Ohio River?"

"We're not going over the Falls of the Ohio?" Woody asked.

"No, sir. We keep our distance from them," the tour guide said.

"OK, then," Woody said as he sat down and looked out the windows on the port side of the boat where he could see the Indiana shore. In the distance, he made out the face of a clock that rose above the shoreline.

"What's that?" he asked.

"That's the world's third biggest clock," the tour guide said. "It used to be the second biggest."

"Why would anyone want to know how much time had passed them by?" Woody said as he turned his head and looked east down the river.

The tour guide lady looked out the window at the face of the huge clock in the distance, checked the time it displayed against the time shown on her cell phone and went back to her post.

THE CRUISE LASTED an hour.

When the boat pulled up to the pier, the crew lowered the gangplank and the passengers disembarked. Woody was the last one left on deck.

"Are you ready to go ashore, Mr. Wilson?" the tour lady asked.

"I reckon so," he said. He glanced around the deck to find something familiar, something red like Maggie wore on special outings like this. When he saw nothing, he lowered his head and walked towards the bow of the ship. The tour guide lady took his right hand with her left and led him down the gangplank onto solid ground.

"It was great to have you with us today, Mr. Wilson. I hope you and Maggie enjoy the rest of your trip," she said.

WHEN WOODY SET foot on the concrete dock, the tour guide handed him off to a couple of deputies, turned and walked back on board the ship. She didn't look back at Woody.

"Mr. Wilson, we're from the sheriff's office. We need to talk with you for a minute," one of them said.

They were each about twenty-five years old with one-inch hair and muscles that bulged out of their short sleeved uniforms like a teen-aged boy's expectations on prom night.

"What can I do for you, officers?" Woody said.

"Your son is worried about you, Mr. Wilson," the shorter deputy said.

"He worries too much," Woody said. "At the Battle of the Bulge, Patton marched us for a week when it was twenty below zero. He could have cared less how we handled it."

The young deputies looked at each other and realized they were talking to a man who had paid his dues, a great man, not grunts like they were.

"You're probably right, Mr. Wilson, but we need to let him know where you are," the taller of the two deputies said. "You'll need to come with us."

Woody walked with them to their cruiser where they opened the rear passenger side door for him. When they had him inside, Woody listened as the taller deputy called dispatch to report that they had him in custody.

A couple of minutes later the deputy's cell rang.

"Yes sir, Mr. Wilson. I'll put him on the line," the deputy said as he handed his cell to Woody.

"Daddy?" a voice said.

"Who else would it be?" Woody said gruffly.

"Momma's been worried about you," his son said. "I'll be there in a little while to pick you up."

"Momma?" Woody said.

"I mean Maggie," his son said.

At the mention of Maggie's name, Woody's face changed; a gleam of light entered his eyes; the harshness faded from his voice. He stroked his fingers through his hair, looked at himself in the rearview mirror to be sure he was presentable.

"Is Maggie coming with you?"

"No, sir. She's at home in Florida waiting for you to make it back," his son said.

"Well then get on down here pronto," Woody said. "I need to get home this evening to see her."

"Yes, sir," the voice on the phone said as he hung up the call.

ON BOARD SHIP, the tour guide lady walked toward the stern until she reached the bar. "Pour me a double. Scotch on the rocks," she said.

When the barkeep handed her the glass, she swirled the liquid in the plastic cup, took a sip. She went out on deck to a spot where she couldn't see Woody and the deputies on the dock and found a chair. When she sat down she could see the face of the giant clock just above the horizon. She finished her drink in one swallow, lifted the empty cup to eye-level and threw it into the muddy water.

"Give 'em hell, Woody Wilson," she said. And she thought about her momma, who had fought her own battle against the disease that stole her mind and stripped her dignity, and she wept alone until the sun sank out of sight and they came and told her it was time to go home.

Chapter 2

NINETY MILES SOUTH in Bowling Green, Woody's son, Waylon, ended the call to his dad.

He appeared younger than his forty-six years, his black hair in a crew cut, his body like that of a marathon runner without the muscle tone. He was five feet nine inches tall, could keyboard at 120 words a minute with his eyes closed, Bach turned up to ten on his headphones. He had small, but not delicate hands, went bare foot in the house.

He stood next to the breakfast bar that separated the kitchen from the den, placed both hands on the granite counter top and hung his head low.

His wife, Jessie, sat at the dining room table 10 feet from her husband. Her 135 pounds barely masked a cheerleader figure. Her brown hair hung down her back curly in moist ringlets from her shower. Her inner drive cast an energy field around her, her mind in overdrive, her look still somehow serene.

She and Waylon had met their junior years at The University of Texas on a blind date. They had been inseparable ever since.

They worked their way from entry level positions, she at an ad agency and he with a startup IT company, through mid-management to executive status. When her company offered her the top job at its Bowling Green branch, she snapped it up, and Waylon decided the move created the perfect opportunity for him to ditch the corporate life style and re-create himself as a full-time computer consultant.

They became empty-nesters two years before when their younger daughter joined her sister at Auburn to double major in football players and Facebook.

Jessie had heard only Waylon's end of the conversation and waited for the verdict.

"He's in Louisville, just like Momma predicted," Waylon said.

"What's he doing there?" she said.

"Momma said they went there on a trip once. She figured he would retrace his steps."

"This has got to stop," Jessie said. "He is going to kill somebody on the road before it's over." She remained seated, looked at the ceiling, then down at the floor.

Waylon walked away from the counter to the plate glass window that opened onto the back yard bordered by an eight foot privacy fence. He watched a brilliant orange Gulf Fritillary butterfly land on a passion flower in the garden and didn't say a word until he saw it flitter away. He looked at Jessie when he spoke.

"I know. I just hate to take his keys away from him. It's about all he has left. We have a lot of years in front of us. He has only darkness ahead of him," he said as his voice cracked.

Jessie looked down at floor. She loved Woody, too.

"I'll drive you to Louisville, and you can bring him back in his truck," she said.

They followed a familiar ritual as they prepared for the trip. They got dressed, set the alarm, let the puppies out into the back yard, filled the dogs' water bowls.

Within ten minutes they were in Jessie's Ford Expedition; she behind the wheel, Waylon quiet in the passenger's seat. They stopped at a convenience store where Waylon got out and walked to the gas pump.

"Do you want anything for the road?" Jessie asked Waylon while he topped off the tank. "I thought I would get some of those little chocolate donuts for Woody. You know how much he loves them."

Waylon put his left arm around her waist for a second, unable to speak. She slipped her right arm inside his, then patted him on the side of his chest, gave him one slight hug and walked across the parking lot as she wiped her eyes with the rolled up sleeve of her brown blouse.

Chapter 3

"WE'RE ON OUR way to pick him up," Waylon reported to Maggie Wilson as he and Jessie sped north on I-65 toward Louisville.

"Be gentle with him, Waylon," Maggie said.

"You know I will, Momma," he said.

"He's been through a lot, Son."

When she hung up the phone, Maggie walked across the living room floor of the condo to the open door that looked out on the sugar white sands of the Florida Panhandle, beaches as familiar to her as her own face, her favorite red dress, her son's laughter.

Born into an Old Florida family that owned ten miles of shoreline before anyone else wanted it, she had wandered these dunes for as long as she could remember. She knew how to catch crabs with bits of bacon tied to string, how to swim parallel to a riptide until it relaxed its deadly grip, where the holes were that harbored pompano, when the cobia would start their run north from the keys and trace their solitary pilgrimage a few yards off the beach as they made their way toward the oil rigs off the Texas coast.

She thought about the changes she had seen the last twenty years when tourists discovered the "Redneck Riviera" as they called it.

They built high-rise condos that blocked everyone else's view of the Gulf and $5,000,000 beach houses that stood vacant fifty weeks out of the year. From scratch just two miles to the west they erected the entire town of Seaside, Florida, with its faux traditions.

She had left the beach when she graduated high school to pursue her dream of becoming a special education teacher. The first woman in her family to go to college, she researched schools all over the nation before she decided to move to San Marcos, Texas, to attend Southwest Texas State Teachers College. She finished first in her class and parlayed that distinction into a first year teaching position at Kilgore High School in the heart of the East Texas oilfield.

That was in 1948.

The news of her arrival spread through the oil patch like a grass fire in August.

At five feet one inch tall, 102 pounds, with hair as dark as a moonless night, skin as white as the congregation at the First Baptist Church, bright red lipstick and luminous blue eyes, she attracted and fended off a horde of roughneck suitors.

That was until one Saturday morning in early November.

She had taken a garage apartment tucked behind one of the big houses of a *nouveau riche* oil family. The back door opened onto a landing at the top of some wooden stairs that was just big enough for one small person.

Polite people always came to the front door.

So she wondered when she heard a knock from the rear of the apartment. She went to the door where through the window she saw a dark-haired mail carrier in his late twenties probably six feet tall with a square chin and a thin face. He had a large box cradled in his arms. Even through the slats of the half-closed venetian blinds, she could see the twinkle in his clear brown eyes, eyes that carried a distant look, almost a look of forgetfulness, as if this young postal worker was engaged in the affairs of another world, while he carried out his duties in this one.

"Special delivery for Margaret Gilbert," the mailman said when he saw her approach the door. He fumbled with the large box, and it struck his cap and knocked it back on his head. He dropped his clipboard and his pencil came loose and slipped through the cracks in the board floor and dropped to the ground.

Maggie opened the door. "I am Margaret Gilbert," she said.

The mailman tried to hand her the box but soon realized that there was not enough room on the landing to make the transfer.

Maggie stepped back inside. "Bring it in and set it on the kitchen table, if you don't mind."

"Yes, ma'am," he said.

He carried it into the kitchen and placed it on the small round oak breakfast table. Then he turned to Maggie.

"Usually we require a signature on a special delivery, but I dropped my pencil," he said. He blushed while he spoke and looked to Maggie's right at the floor.

"You'd think someone like me would have a pencil here

somewhere. But I believe I am all out of them right now," Maggie said. "I am a school teacher, you know."

"Everybody in town knows that, I reckon," he said still afraid to look her in the eye.

"I am at a disadvantage here, sir," she said.

"Pardon me, ma'am?"

"You know my name, but I don't know yours."

The postal worker took off his cap with his right hand, slicked his curly black hair back with his left and finally made eye contact.

"I'm Woodrow Wilson, Miss Gilbert. But folks around here call me Woody."

"The kids at school call me Miss Gilbert, my folks call me Margaret Ann, but you may call me Maggie," she said.

"I am very pleased to meet you, Maggie," Woody said.

They shook hands and Woody held on just a little longer than he would if he had shaken the hand of another man. Her hand fit into his like a child's hand fits into the pocket of a first baseman's mitt. He released his firm, gentle grip.

"I guess I better be on my way, Maggie. I have a lot of stops to make today. I'll need to come back and get your signature for the special delivery. When would be a good time?"

"How about seven tonight?" she asked.

"I'll be through with my shift by then," he said.

"I figured as much."

Woody stood a few feet from her and didn't move while he processed her words. Then a grin broke out on his face; he put his cap on his head and turned toward the door. Just before he closed it behind him, he said through the crack, "I'll see you at seven, Maggie."

She listened as he vaulted down the steps.

Through the window, she watched him retrieve his pencil from the dirt, stick it in his pocket and race toward the street.

Emerald waves lapped against the beach as the sun almost disappeared below the horizon, the horizon Woody loved to watch from their balcony as he smoked his pipe and cackled under his breath about the tourists.

"You'd think they would know they are making shark bait of themselves," he would say.

She just wanted to sit next to him again, to put her hand in his. She loved to watch the wonder in his eyes as he said, "It's a pretty place, ain't it, Maggie?" for the thousandth time as he strained to see as far out to sea as he could.

"Beautiful," she would say.

Chapter 4

AT TEN-THIRTY THE next morning Maggie arrived at BWG, the airport in Bowling Green, Kentucky. When she entered the terminal, Waylon and Jessie were standing there with Woody.

"Hey, doll face," Woody said when he saw her. He grabbed her around the waist and gave her a big kiss on the lips.

"Am I glad to see you. The folks I have been staying with here were a drag," Woody said as he leaned next to her to whisper in her ear.

Jessie relaxed her grip on Maggie's right hand when she overheard Woody's remark. Maggie looked her in the eye to let her know it was all right.

"You want to visit the Corvette Museum?" Woody asked Maggie.

"Sounds like fun," Maggie said. "I have to get my bag from baggage claim. Then we can check it out."

Woody looked around at the signs that were everywhere

in the terminal. "I think it's this way," he said, starting to walk toward the exit.

"I need to go to the lady's room first," Maggie said as she took his hand and directed him the opposite way. "Wait for me, and we can walk down to the baggage area together."

"I'll stand guard," Woody said.

While Maggie was in the ladies' room, Woody said his goodbyes.

"Thanks for your help, young man," he told his son, not quite able to bring up his name. "I appreciate the hospitality," he said to no one in particular although he nodded in Jessie's general direction.

"Any time, Mr. Woody," Jessie said. She backed away from him just far enough to leave him alone with Waylon.

"You got a good one there, boy," Woody said as he looked over at Jessie. "Although I can't quite figure out what she sees in you." His eyes twinkled like they did when he used to play Santa Claus for the Lion's Club.

"No telling, Dad. I stopped trying to figure women out a long time ago," Waylon said.

"Me, too. There's no future in it," Woody said as he poked his son in the side with his elbow. "God didn't give us a clue about that. Can't live with 'em; can't live without 'em." He winked at Waylon and walked closer to the entrance to the ladies' room to wait for Maggie.

Waylon and Jessie waited for Maggie to come out. When she did, they waved at her and pointed toward the spot in the parking lot where they had left Woody's truck.

Maggie flashed her eyes at them and took Woody's hand again. She watched as Waylon escorted Jessie to their Ford Expedition.

"Let's go to the museum," she said. "I always liked those '57 Corvettes."

"Like the one I used to race along the river when you sat shotgun?" he said.

"You know it," Maggie said.

They found his truck in the parking lot and Woody threw her luggage in the bed. He opened the passenger door for her and shut it gently behind her when she stepped up into the cab.

"You're not going to believe all the 'Vettes they have here, Maggie," he said.

He drove his truck out of the airport and made his way to I-65 North.

Maggie scooted next to him on the bench seat and laid her head on his shoulder. She rested her left hand on his right leg. Woody reached down with his right hand and grasped her hand like he was afraid she might run away.

"Sweetheart, you know you have to quit running off like that, don't you? You scared Waylon to death. He thought he had lost you for good. Your trip up here was supposed to be an adventure for you, but not a chance for you to run away," Maggie said.

"I know I shouldn't do stuff like that, Maggie," Woody said. "But I had a dream that he and his girl friend were getting ready to take my keys away from me, rob me and dump me on the side of the road."

"That girl friend is Jessie. They've been married twenty-two years and are the parents of our two grandchildren," Maggie said.

"They both love you and would never do anything to hurt you."

In a few minutes, they saw the distinctive yellow dome with its spiral reaching towards the sky on the west side of the Interstate that advertised in bold color the hot rod museum.

"I won't let it happen again; I promise," Woody said as he exited and turned left towards the Corvette shrine.

"Scout's honor?" Maggie asked.

"Cross my heart and hope to die," Woody said.

Maggie leaned over, kissed him and patted his leg.

"You'll always be my hero, Woodrow Wilson," she said.

Woody let Maggie out at the museum entrance, parked his truck and joined her in the ticket line. He fumbled around in his billfold for some money and became agitated when he came up empty.

"This is my treat," Maggie said as she handed the clerk the entrance fee.

"Thank you, ma'am," Woody said as he bowed towards Maggie. "Lunch is on me, baby."

"Deal," she said.

"It's time for me to powder my nose for a minute, Woodrow Wilson," Maggie said when they got into the main exhibit hall.

"I'll be right over there," Woody said as he pointed at some of the cars.

"See you in a minute," Maggie said.

In the powder room, Maggie took out her cell and called Waylon. "We're at the Corvette Museum. We'll come by your place when we get through here. Thanks for all you are doing," she told him.

"Of course, Momma," Waylon said. "He loves the 'Vette museum. I hope you brought some comfortable shoes. You may be there a while."

She took a compact from her purse and dabbed a little powder on her face, a face that looked ten years younger than her eighty-three years, save for the crows' feet of worry that had crept into the corners of her eyes the last three years, years she had trailed Woody from place to place, keeping him out of trouble, making amends where they were needed. She walked out the door less than two minutes from when she entered. Near the exit of the women's room, a young black man stood with a piece of paper in his hand.

"Mrs. Wilson?" he asked when she came out.

"Yes."

"Mr. Wilson asked me to give you this," he said as he handed her a folded note.

The note read: "Waylon and his girl friend are trying to lock me up. They will have to catch me first. Don't forget how much I love you, Maggie."

It was signed "Woody."

"Where did he go?" Maggie asked the young man as the old panic returned, the worry that she had seen the love of her life for the last time.

He shrugged and walked away.

Maggie went to the window that looked out on the parking lot just in time to see Woody's truck as it pulled out of the museum grounds and headed for the entrance ramp to I-65 South.

Woody stuck his left hand out the driver's side window and waved as he rounded the corner, the corner where the traffic light had turned red ahead of him. He turned right at the light and floored the accelerator as he merged into the traffic and barreled south toward Nashville on the Interstate at nearly eighty miles per hour.

"Oh, Woody, what am I going to do with you?" Maggie said as she watched until his truck was out of sight. She started to run to the nearest security guard and explain the situation, seek his help. But something deep inside of her held her back. She knew Woody stood at the point of no return. She could have him back, but at the cost of his freedom. He could stay at large, perhaps at the cost of his life.

She made her decision.

She strolled around the museum and waited for twenty minutes before she took out her cell and called Waylon.

"I went in the restroom to powder my nose and when I came out I couldn't find him," she said. "My guess is that he is headed back toward Florida this time."

"I'll call the highway patrol," Waylon said. "I'll be there to get you in about fifteen minutes."

"Okay, Son."

"Momma?" Waylon said.

"Yes."

"You know we will have to ground him when we catch him this time, don't you?"

"I know, son," she said. "Let me handle it when the time comes."

"Yes, ma'am," Waylon said.

Maggie found a '57 'Vette and stood next to it while she waited for Waylon.

"We made quite the fine couple in that old Corvette, Mr. Woody," she said to herself. She thought about the late August nights fifty years before when the temperature was still near ninety degrees at ten o'clock, evenings when they put the top down and, for the next day's bragging rights, raced all comers up and down the main highway that ran through Kilgore, Texas.

And she remembered how after the racing played out, she and Woody would ride out to the lake after midnight, park the 'Vette near the water at the marina and listen to the wind as it caused the boats to creak against their moorings. Finally Woody would say, "Morning is going to come early for a school teacher and a mailman," and they would kiss and Woody would start the car and drive slowly along the back roads until they came to their two bedroom frame house that backed up to the elementary school playground.

"That was the best day I ever had, Maggie," Woody would say as he dropped off for a few hours of sleep.

"Me, too," she would say as she moved her body against him, a perfect fit.

Chapter 5

OFFICER SHERWOOD REYNOLDS of the Nashville PD sat at his desk in an efficiency apartment in a rundown part of town and cleaned his Smith and Wesson Model 686 .357-caliber revolver in preparation for another day on the street. He put his thumb next to the end of the six-inch barrel near the cylinder and held the gun so that the light from his desk lamp reflected off his thumbnail. He looked through the front of the barrel to check that the rifling was clean. He took an oilcloth, wiped the weapon one more time, laid it on the desk.

At fifty-two years of age he had been the department's chief detective for ten years until his steady on-the-job drinking caught up with him, and he got busted to a patrol unit three years before. It was the same drinking that cost him his marriage and made his only daughter a stranger, then an enemy.

His six-feet-two inch frame carried 225 pounds of muscle trimmed with a donut of fat around his mid-section that lopped over his belt even if he held his stomach in when he walked. His brown hair had streaks of gray that accented the wrinkles on his forehead and the bags under his eyes.

The top marksman in the department for fifteen years running, he had noticed in the last two months a tremor that crept into his hand as he tried to hold the heavy pistol steady, a tremor that made any shot a challenge, especially shots made under the pressure of life and death situations.

He slipped the pistol into a holster and left it on the desk top while he shaved and put on his uniform. The last thing before he walked out of the apartment, he put his gun on his belt and looked at himself in the floor length mirror that hung from the bathroom door.

"I make this look good," he said as he shook his head in disbelief at the mess he had made of his life.

Shortly before nightfall, Reynolds pulled his patrol unit up on a truck he thought matched a "be-on-the-lookout" advisory. It was in the parking lot of the Hyatt Place Hotel near Opryland.

He flashed his lights and saw no movement in the cab. He got out. "Nashville PD," he yelled.

In the fading light, he drew his large metal flashlight and shined the beam in the cab. In the compartment behind the front seat, he saw half-full water bottles, McDonald's wrappers and banana peels.

He walked across the parking lot and entered the lobby of the hotel. "I'm Officer Reynolds with Nashville PD," he said as he flashed his badge at the front desk.

"Do you have a guest by this name registered here?" He showed the clerk a copy of Woody's driver's license that accompanied the "be on the lookout" alert.

The clerk, a young woman not quite twenty, smiled at the policeman.

"Do you know the magic word?" she teased.

Reynolds played along.

"Please," he said.

"All right, I'll check," she said.

She punched a couple of keys on her computer and furrowed her brow. Then she hit a few more keys.

"It shows here that he was scheduled to check in yesterday, but he never arrived," she said. "He didn't call to cancel his reservation."

"Can you tell whether he booked the room on-line?"

"It looks like someone booked it for him, but I don't have access to the information because it was through a third party Internet site. Anything else, officer?" She seemed impressed with her own efficiency.

"Just one thing. If he shows up, can you give me a call?" He handed her his card.

"You bet. Maybe I'll call you even if he doesn't show up," she said.

"You'll have to use your own judgment on that, ma'am," Reynolds said as he tipped his hat to her. He walked outside to Woody's truck and looked it over from several angles. Then he called it in. "I have the truck that matches the BOLO," he told the dispatcher. "Better send a crew out here to process the scene."

"Stay put, Reynolds," the dispatcher said. "They're having a slow night. Someone should be there in a few minutes."

Within half an hour the crime scene investigators swarmed the parking lot, taking pictures, dusting for fingerprints, bagging the food items in the truck.

"It's not all that complicated is it?" Reynolds asked the CSI in charge.

"What do you mean?"

"I saw two sets of footprints next to the truck. The clerk told me someone made the reservation for him. So whoever made the reservation decided they would save him a night's lodging at a hotel and take him home with him or her instead. Mr. Wilson thought it made sense to him, so he never checked in the hotel. I guess he abandoned the truck and figured his family would come and get it when we called them," Reynolds said.

The CSI thought about it.

"Makes sense all right, except for one thing."

"What's that?"

"Wilson is supposed to be an Alzheimer's patient. What you are describing would take some planning, which I doubt he could do."

"Have you ever lived around an Alzheimer's patient?" Reynolds asked.

"No."

"I wish I hadn't. Until they reach a certain stage, they may have long periods of cogency before they fall back into dementia. His mind could have cleared long enough to pull this off."

"Sounds like you learned it the hard way," the CSI said.

"My dad," Reynolds said. "I watched him fight it for ten years. I'd rather take my chances in a small boat on the open sea when the time comes."

The CSI thought about Reynolds' words. They were about the same age.

"I told my kids if they see it coming they are supposed

to tell me, 'Daddy, your memory is not what it used to be.' That will be my cue. I hope I have the courage then to launch my twenty-two footer into the Gulf and turn it towards the southern horizon."

"Problem is, we never know if we'll be up to it when the time comes," Reynolds said.

The two men looked at each other for a minute before their thoughts drifted back to the crime scene.

"Maybe the friend knew about the Alzheimer's and figured he was the guy's guardian angel," the CSI said.

"Maybe so, but it could just have easily been someone who realized he could take him to the cleaners before he recognized what was happening to him," Reynolds said.

"Then I guess we better find him before that happens," the CSI said.

"Roger that," Reynolds said.

Chapter 6

ON THE EVENING of the third day of Woody's disappearance, Waylon and Maggie Wilson met Officer Reynolds as he came out of the precinct house on his way home.

"Officer Reynolds."

"Yes ma'am."

"I'm Maggie Wilson. This is my son Waylon. We are looking for Woody Wilson and I understand you are the man who found his truck," Maggie said. "We aren't getting much information from anyone at Nashville PD."

"It's in the hands of the detectives, Ms. Wilson. I'm just the guy in the patrol car," Reynolds said.

Maggie looked him up and down. Her blues eyes examined the details of his uniform, the way his hair curled into ringlets, the slight scuffs on his black Justin Roper boots, the extra notch he had gouged into his belt with a pocket knife to give himself some breathing room. When she finished her inspection, she moved a step closer to him and looked him in the eye. "I doubt that, Officer Reynolds," she said. "Something tells me you have more experience in law enforcement than most guys on patrol."

Reynolds locked his gaze on her. He liked her immediately. She wasn't the sort of lady anyone could bullshit.

"If you had access to my personnel file, you would see some things that worked against me professionally," he said. "Not the least of which was ten years or so of heavy drinking, much of it on the clock."

"But you're not drinking now, are you?" Maggie wouldn't let him look away.

"No ma'am. I figured I was either going to have to give it up or turn pro. So three years ago I gave it up."

Waylon moved a step closer to Reynolds.

"So what's happened to daddy, in your professional opinion, Officer Reynolds?"

"I think someone he knows has him hid out somewhere," Reynolds said. "Since we haven't received any ransom calls and the body hasn't showed up, I figure the person may be trying to sort out his next move. Your dad is probably content to let it play out right now, probably thinks it is some sort of vacation trip. Sooner or later he's going to get nervous and make a run for it. I give him a couple of more days."

"I've spent more than sixty years with Woody Wilson, Officer Reynolds," Maggie said. "That's the way I see it, too. I would like for you to be involved personally in this case. Can we make some sort of arrangement to retain you as a private investigator? I want you on our team."

Reynolds looked at both of them, his head cocked a little off center, his hands on his hips, a faraway look in his eyes.

"You can't pay me, Mrs. Wilson," he said. "But you have my word that I am on the case and won't quit 'til we find Mr. Wilson." He reached out and shook hands with Maggie, her firm grip conveying all the secrets of life to him in a heartbeat, all the values he cherished in human beings, all the things missing from his wrecked life.

"By the way, Mrs. Wilson, my name is Sherwood Reynolds, but most people around here call me by my nickname," Reynolds said.

"What's that, Sherwood?" Maggie asked.

"Shot Glass," Reynolds said.

"I should have seen that one coming, Sherwood," Maggie said as she squeezed his hand one more time, turned and walked across the parking lot to her car.

Reynolds grinned as he watched Waylon and her pull out into the street.

Chapter 7

"SHOT GLASS," THE dispatcher said when Reynolds returned to duty after two days off.

"Yeah?"

"Captain wants to see you."

"What's up?"

"He didn't say, but he sounded like he might have a cob up his ass about something."

"Sounds like a good way to start the work week," Reynolds said.

Reynolds walked down a hall framed with plate glass windows behind which he could see Nashville's finest as they worked at their desks. They made phone calls, tried to look busy with important matters. Some of them nodded at him as he passed; others shot him the finger.

"Go on in, Shot Glass," the captain's secretary said when she saw Reynolds. "You're looking mighty fine this morning, Rosalee," Reynolds said to her on his way in.

"You're not looking too bad yourself for an old man," Rosalee replied as she swiveled in her chair and watched him through the captain's door.

"Close it," Captain Walker said. He pointed his right index finger at the door like a patrol officer would direct traffic around a bad wreck on a hot summer afternoon.

Reynolds shut the door and sat down in a straight-backed metal chair in front of the captain's desk.

"You wanted to see me, captain?"

"What do you know about the Wilson investigation?" Walker asked.

"Middle of last week I found Woody Wilson's truck and called it in. The facts seemed to indicate to me that someone who knew he was coming met him at the Hyatt Place Hotel and took him in or kidnapped him. His wife and son came to see me a couple of days ago, and I told them I would do whatever I could to help them find Woody. That's about it," Reynolds said.

"Well, it seems like someone in the Wilson family has made some calls to some powerful people who, for whatever reason, have taken a keen interest in the case," Walker said.

"I guess that's good," Reynolds said.

"Let's hope so. I don't know if you've seen the papers, but the governor has recently agreed to serve as a national chairperson for the Alzheimer's Network, a group devoted to upgrading our ability to locate and save Alzheimer's patients who lose their bearings."

"Sounds like another good thing," Reynolds said.

"Except for the fact that a lot of press about a missing Alzheimer's patient in his home state makes the governor look bad," Walker said.

"His office wants us to make Woody Wilson's disappearance a top priority."

"Sounds like another good thing," Reynolds said.

"Will you stop saying that?" Walker said.

"What would you like for me to say, Chief?" Reynolds said.

"Just keep your mouth shut for a minute.

"I know you have some experience dealing with Alzheimer's. I also know you are a hell of a detective when you're sober. Apparently Mrs. Wilson has made a specific request for your services in this case, and as a courtesy to the governor's office, I plan to oblige her. As of now, you are off patrol and on special assignment as detective in charge of the investigation," Walker said.

"With detective pay?" Reynolds asked.

"Don't push your luck, Shot Glass," Walker said as he stood up behind his desk.

Reynolds knew that meant the meeting was over. He had one more thing to add. "I think I know where Mr. Wilson is, captain," Reynolds said.

The captain looked at him like he knew he shouldn't take the bait. He took it anyway. "Where's that?"

"He's with the hundreds of thousands of people from the greatest generation who reside near the intersection of World War Two and Alzheimer's. The main boulevard at that location is a one way street," Reynolds said.

"You're a hard man to figure, Reynolds," Walker said. He picked up a pencil and made a note on the outside of a manila file folder that lay on his desk. He looked at Reynolds.

"I want a daily direct report. Find Wilson and bring him back to his family. And do it in a hurry."

"I'll do my best, Captain."

"I'm counting on that, Reynolds." Walker slapped a badge marked 'special investigator' in his hand and shut the door behind him.

Reynolds flashed the badge at Rosalee as he walked past her desk. She smiled and gave him a thumbs up.

As he walked down the hall, he let the badge dangle from his jacket pocket so everyone could see it. Without turning to look back over his shoulder at anyone in the squad room, he waved his middle finger in the air just before he walked around the corner out of their field of view.

Chapter 8

WHILE REYNOLDS TRANSFERRED his gear from his patrol car to his new unmarked vehicle, his cell rang.

"Officer Reynolds," a young girl's voice said. "This is Alicia."

"Alicia?" Reynolds said.

"From the Hyatt Place. You gave me a card and asked me to call if I had any news about the guy whose truck you found in the parking lot," she said.

"Woody Wilson," Reynolds said.

"Whatever," Alicia said.

"So what have you got for me, Alicia?"

"It may not amount to anything, but one of the guys from housekeeping told me he thought he saw another dude talking to Woody Wilson earlier that day."

"Where's the guy from housekeeping now?"

"His shift ends at three o'clock this afternoon."

"Tell him to sit tight. I'll be there in about twenty minutes,"

Reynolds said.

"Don't forget to drop by and say hi to me while you're in the neighborhood," Alicia said with a giggle.

Shot Glass hung up the phone.

THE GUY FROM housekeeping was a sixty-three year old white guy who had spent most of his adult life in the state hospital hearing voices in his head. A month earlier state budget cuts turned him out on the street with a strong prescription for Valium and no way to pay for it. He wore a dirty pair of brown Dickies slacks and a Hyatt Place short sleeve shirt. He hadn't washed his hair in a week and he smelled like the dumpster where he dumped the hotel's garbage three times a day.

He gave his name to Shot Glass as Enrico Fermi.

"Is it Mr. or Dr. Fermi?" Reynolds asked him as he took notes.

"Just call me Enrico," he said.

"What did you see, Enrico?"

"I was taking a load to the dumpster about four o'clock and saw the truck the PD searched in the parking lot. An old guy was sitting in the cab, and another guy a little younger, maybe about your age, was standing next to the driver's window talking to him."

Shot Glass let the age remark pass.

"What else, Enrico?"

"They were talking to each other like they were friends. In a few minutes, the guy in the truck ..."

"His name is Mr. Wilson," Reynolds said.

"Mr. Wilson got out of his vehicle with a small suit case under his arm and followed the other guy to his car. They both got in and took off that way," he said. He pointed to his right, toward Opryland.

"Could you hear any of their conversation?"

"No, I was too far away. But I figure I heard it already," Fermi said.

"Why do you say that, Enrico?"

"I knew the other guy. He's a shrink at the state hospital where I used to see patients," Enrico said.

"I thought you were a nuclear physicist?" Shot Glass said.

"That was before I started my physicist career," Enrico said.

"What's this shrink's name?"

"We all just called him Doc Smooth. You know, because he kept us smoothed out all the time. He passed out pills like they were candy."

"Anything else, Enrico?"

"That's it, Officer Reynolds. There is one thing though," he said.

"What's that?"

"Could you loan me enough money for a pack of smokes?"

Shot Glass stuck a ten spot in Enrico's hand and watched as he walked across the street to a discount tobacco store.

ON HIS WAY back to the station house, Reynolds got out his cell. "Maggie, it's Shot Glass," he said.

"Did you find him, Sherwood?"

She sounded worried, tired.

"Not yet. I need to ask you a question."

"I'll do whatever I can to help," she said.

"Does Woody know any psychiatrists here in Tennessee?"

"Not to my knowledge. But he has a lot of friends from the service that he keeps up with occasionally, and he used to attend veterans meetings around the country. I suppose he could have met a doctor there. But I never heard him mention it," she said.

"This guy probably isn't old enough to be a World War Two vet. Anything else come to mind?"

"Well, he has a psychiatrist friend in Panama City that he invites to go boating with him, but so far as I know that doctor has no connection to Tennessee," Maggie said.

"What's his name?"

"I just met him in passing a couple of times at the marina, but I think it was a strange German name, like Schmutscher or something along those lines," she said. "Woody just calls him Doc Smooth, but I thought he made that up."

"Maybe not," Reynolds said. "I have a lead I am working on. I'll get back with you as soon as I know something."

"Thanks, Sherwood."

"You're welcome, Maggie."

AT THE STATION Reynolds found a spare desk in the corner and Googled the Middle Tennessee Mental Health Institute in Nashville. He couldn't find a list of shrinks, so he called the main number.

"Mental Health Institute," the receptionist said.

"Yes, ma'am, this is Detective Reynolds, Nashville PD. I'm trying to find out if you have psychiatrist on staff there that calls himself 'Doc Smooth,'" he said.

"They all think they are smooth, detective. If you ask me, they are just a bunch of overpaid lardasses who couldn't get a real job," she said.

"Sounds like some cops I know," Reynolds said.

The receptionist laughed into the phone.

"I like your attitude, Reynolds," she said.

"And I like yours, Ms..,"

"Ms. Theodora Dixon," she said. "I've been cleaning up messes out here for going on twenty years. I call 'em like I see 'em."

"Me, too, Ms. Dixon. Now who is Doc Smooth?"

"Linus Schmutzer. He's here on sabbatical from some medical facility in Florida. One of our regular docs swapped places with him for a year."

"How long has he been at your place?"

"He started about two months ago. But if you count the days he's actually here, he has put in about a week. He's milking this deal for everything it's worth. People like me have to punch the clock," she said.

"I'm looking for a missing person, Ms. Dixon. A white guy in his early eighties, thin, sort of quiet, gray stubble of a beard most of the time. Has anybody been admitted to your facility in the last week that meets that description? I have some sketchy information that seems to indicate he may be either a patient or an acquaintance of Doc Smooth's."

"Nope. We are full up right now. No new patients for the last three weeks," Theodora said. "I've never seen anybody with Doc Smooth while he was on campus, other than our inmates."

"When is Doc Smooth supposed to be on the premises again?" Reynolds said.

"He is supposed to be here now, but I haven't seen him all week. You want his home address and cell phone number?"

"You're a woman after my own heart, Theodora," Reynolds said.

"I bet you tell that to all the girls at the state hospital," she said.

From the left pocket of his shirt, Reynolds pulled out his pocket-sized notepad and wrote down the address and cell as she read them off to him. The residence address was in Franklin, twenty miles south of Nashville.

"Ms. Dixon, if I give you my number, will you buzz me the next time the good doctor graces you with his presence? And by the way, most of my friends call me Shot Glass," he said.

"Sounds like something I could have called a couple of my ex-husbands," Theodora said.

"I quit three years ago," Reynolds said. "But some things follow you around for a while."

"We all need a chance to start over, Shot Glass. I can tell already that you have put your feet back on the right path. Drop by and see me when you come to visit the doc."

"You can count on it, Theodora," Reynolds said as he ended the call.

"Looks like it is time for a little surveillance work," Reynolds said. He poured the last dregs of day old coffee from the squad room pot into a sixteen ounce Styrofoam cup, bought some peanut butter crackers from the vending machine in the hall, went out the sally port and hopped in his new Crown Vic.

By the time the sun set behind the middle Tennessee hills, he was perched on the side of the road, his binoculars in hand, sweeping his gaze over a hundred acres of pasture and oak trees that shrouded a century-old farm house, the farm house, that according to the Williamson county deed records, had belonged to the Schmutzer family for 140 years.

Chapter 9

JESSIE WILSON KNELT on the hard pine floor of her attic
and sifted through pictures stored in an old trunk, pictures of
the things she had loved the most, the hardest, for the longest
time. Woody popped up in many, if not most, of them, always
smiling, almost grinning, as if life tickled him.

In one taken on her wedding day, Woody stood
beaming next to Waylon, his best man. In another he held
Jessie's first born at the hospital.

There was one of him serving as a pallbearer at her
dad's funeral, crying next to the grave while she and Waylon
stood on either side of him, an arm draped over his shoulder,
their heads hung low, in a misty cold December rain two weeks
before her baby girl's first Christmas.

Soon she wept, too. Not because Woody was lost, but
because of what they had lost of Woody. She remembered on
her wedding day, just before Waylon and she ran out of the
church fellowship hall to get in the car and start their weekend

honeymoon sandwiched between low-paying jobs, how he had taken her aside, in private, and placed an envelope in her hand.

"Put this in your purse, my new daughter," he told her. "Waylon doesn't have much money, but he has all the love in the world." Later at the motel she drew it out and showed it to Waylon, the five crisp hundred dollar bills looking for all the world to them like a king's ransom and they laughed, then cried, then called Woody collect to thank him and he laughed and cried, too.

She daubed the tears from her eyes with the tail of Waylon's old white cotton shirt that she wore when she did chores around the house, and her gaze fell on an aged over-sized manila envelope wrapped around with a rubber band.

"I don't remember this," she said as she took it and peeled the band off. It cracked and burst at her first tug. In Maggie's unmistakable flowing hand were written with a fountain pen on the outside of the envelope "Fall, 1957."

Inside Jessie found a half-dozen black and white photos of a younger Woody and Maggie on a road trip in a Corvette, the top down, their faces sunburned, Woody grinning, Maggie smiling with her mouth open. Among shots of burger joints where girls on roller skates waited on them while they sat in their car, old buildings that looked somehow historic and an Amish couple riding in a horse-drawn surrey, one especially caught her eye.

In the photo there was a third person, a man some years older than Woody dressed in a wool sports jacket, the knot of his tie perfectly formed, snugged up against his pressed white cotton shirt, his dark wool slacks draped over a slender, almost emaciated frame, his leather two-toned shoes polished to a brilliant sheen. The man sat between Woody and Maggie with his arms around their necks, pulling them close to him so the unknown photographer could catch all three of them.

In the background, Jessie saw large oaks surrounding a farm house set in the country. A horse grazed in the pasture oblivious to them. At the bottom edge of the picture, Jessie could make out the outline of a woman's long skirt in the shadow that fell on the driver's side rear tire of the Corvette.

Jessie gently stuffed the pictures back in the envelope, wrapped a linen pillowcase around it to protect it and placed it in the bottom of the trunk.

She took her cell from her shirt pocket and called Maggie.

"Good morning, Ms. Maggie," she said. "How are you holding up today?"

They had invited Maggie to stay with them for a few days to see if Woody turned up someplace nearby, but she had declined their offer, choosing rather to take a room at the Courtyard by Marriot. "Good fences make good neighbors," she said.

"I'm hanging in there, baby," Maggie said. "I got a call yesterday from Sherwood. He said he was working a lead of some sort, so I have my fingers crossed."

Jessie told her about the package of photos she found.

"It said the Fall of 1957?" Maggie asked.

"Yes, ma'am."

"I remember that trip, now. We had just bought the Corvette, and Woody wanted to test it out, so we piled in it and let the road take us where it would," Maggie said. "We logged a couple of thousand miles in about three days."

"Where did the road take you?" Jessie asked.

"We were living in Kilgore, Texas, so we got up at the

crack of dawn and drove to Little Rock, spent the next night in Nashville, turned south outside of town and winded our way home. I remember the narrow bridge across the Mississippi at Vicksburg on the old highway. This was long before there were any Interstates. We met an eighteen wheeler. I'll bet there weren't three inches of clearance between him and us."

"Maggie, there is one picture of the two of you with a man in a sports jacket and tie. It looks like you were visiting him at some place in the country."

There was a pause on the line as Maggie thought about it. "Jessie, I need to call Sherwood. I'll call you back," she said as she hung up the phone in a hurry.

Jessie looked at her cell for a minute and said a quick prayer for Woody. Then she backed down the collapsible ladder out of the attic and raised it to cover the access hole in the ceiling. The large spring slammed the door shut and rattled the light fixtures.

Chapter 10

"SHERWOOD?" MAGGIE SAID.

"Yes ma'am."

"It's Maggie Wilson."

"Yes ma'am."

"Jessie just called me with some information that jogged my memory," she said.

"What is it?"

"Woody and I took a trip in the fall of 1957 to Nashville. On the way home, we stopped at a place a little south of town and visited with a friend of Woody's from the war."

"Can you be any more specific about the location?"

"It was a farm house surrounded by pastures and old oak trees. Woody's friend was a nephew or something of the family and was visiting there for a while," she said.

"How old was his friend?" Reynolds asked.

"I would think he was in his mid-forties, ten years or so older than Woody."

"Since that was over fifty years ago, he would be in his 90s now," Reynolds said. "That's a lot older than the person a witness puts with Woody at the hotel."

Reynolds could tell that this news disappointed Maggie. He could hear her starting to cry.

"Don't let it upset you, Maggie. This information is still helpful. I traced the person of interest to a farm that meets your description in Franklin, a town south of Nashville." Reynolds continued, "I set up surveillance last night, but the place looks deserted right now. I checked with the Williamson county sheriff's office, and they say the Schmutzer family still owns and maintains the place. Various family members visit from time to time. The deputies go out there every so often and check the locks to be sure no one has vandalized it."

"Well, at least that's something," Maggie said as she regained her composure.

"I'll go back out there this evening and watch the place," Reynolds said. "Is there anything else you can tell me about Woody's friend?"

"Woody was always secretive about him, as he was about a lot of things from the war. I got the impression that the man had encountered many hardships during the war, hardships too painful to discuss, things better left unexamined."

"It's not uncommon for that to happen, Maggie," Reynolds said. "I've seen some things I'd rather not discuss, too."

"I'll bet you have, Sherwood," Maggie said.

"I'll call when I know something," Reynolds said.

On his way to Franklin that evening, Reynolds got another call.

"Shot Glass?" It was Theodora Dixon.

"Yes, Ms. Dixon," Sherwood said.

"Doc Smooth came in just before my shift ended this evening. I tried to stall him, but he seemed to be in a big hurry. He blew past me at the reception desk, went in his office and came out in a couple of minutes with a briefcase under one arm and a bunch of file folders under the other."

"Did he say anything?"

"He said he had an emergency back home and wasn't sure when, or if, he would be back," she said.

"Good riddance, huh?" Reynolds said.

"My thoughts exactly," Theodora said. "And there's one other thing."

"Go on."

"He parked his car next to the front door. I could see an old man sitting in the front passenger seat. He looked like he might be sleeping."

"Or drugged?" Reynolds said.

"Or drugged," Theodora said.

"What kind of car?"

"A 2010 black Subaru Outback. At six-thirty this evening, he turned south on I-65 at mile marker 87. Would you like the license plate number?"

Reynolds wrote down the tag number.

"Have you ever considered a career in law enforcement, Theodora?" Reynolds said. He could hear Theodora laughing as she ended the call.

Chapter 11

LINUS SCHMUTZER II caught a glimpse of Theodora Dixon tailing him to the entrance ramp of I-65 South.

"You old biddy," he said. "Why don't you mind your own business?"

"What'd you say?" Woody mumbled from the passenger's seat, his eyes closed. His head rested against the back of the seat.

"Nothing, Mr. Woody," Linus said. "I was just venting a little road rage." Schmutzer waited until he was sure that Theodora didn't follow him onto the Interstate, drove to the second exit, turned off and made his way through the back streets to his destination.

He pulled up next to an old warehouse in a rundown part of town, got out of the car and unlocked the padlock on the chain on the gate. A six foot chain link fence topped with barbed-wire enclosed the grounds. He shut the gate, locked it behind him and drove around the back of the building. He unlocked a sliding metal door and pushed it far enough to the side so that he could drive his car in. Once inside, he slid the door closed, threw the latch to secure himself inside and looked around.

On the bare concrete floor of the warehouse, he saw more than a dozen vintage automobiles draped with individual covers. He went to one and yanked the tarp off it. It was a 1956 Chrysler Imperial in perfect condition, push-button transmission, air-conditioned, even a turntable under the dash.

"This one will do," Schmutzer said. "Uncle Linus always knew how to pick 'em."

Linus went to the Subaru and helped Woody out of the seat. He opened the back passenger side door of the Chrysler and laid Woody down on the back seat.

"Where are we going, Doc Smooth?" Woody said.

"We're going to see Maggie, Mr. Woody," Linus said.

"That's good. I can't wait to see that girl," Woody said as he dropped off to sleep.

Linus reached for his medical bag on the floorboard. He felt around in it and pulled out a bottle that contained a premixed solution of propofol and lidocaine, the cocktail that killed Michael Jackson. He filled a syringe with the medicine, unbuttoned Woody's shirt sleeve and exposed his bicep. He swabbed the skin with an alcohol pad, inserted the thin needle into Woody's arm and injected Woody with the full dose of the anesthetic and painkiller.

"Sleep tight, Mr. Woody," he said.

He went out the same way he came in, leaving the warehouse gates locked behind him. As it began to get dark, he stayed off the main roads as he moved ever farther south, toward Montgomery, Alabama, where he knew he would intersect Highway 331 about midnight.

He hoped to be in his own bed in the Florida Panhandle before sunrise.

WHILE DOC SMOOTH drove, Woody Wilson, free for a while from the constraints of his otherwise shackled brain, stalked the Ardennes in search of German werewolves, the lone assassins who slit the throats of GIs with long field knives while they stood guard duty at night in the frozen forest. He positioned himself next to a tree and waited. In a moment he heard a crack as the assassin stepped on a branch, a branch the other end of which was lodged under Woody's boot. Woody held his breath, clenched his rifle next to him, prepared to ram the butt of the stock into the killer's chest.

He knew his only hope was to knock him down and strangle him with his bare hands. The probable outcome of such a struggle would be his own death, for the werewolf was trained for such a moment. He would revel in it as he beat Woody back and stuck him like a pig with his bayonet. He would stand over him and watch until Woody bled out in a crimson splotch of snowy death.

Just before Woody started his lunge, he heard the snow crackle under the feet of the werewolf as he moved away from the trunk of the tree. The sound of his footfalls faded into the icy wind until they fell silent. Woody counted to a thousand before he dared to peek around the other side of the tree. He saw the footprints as they trailed away toward another GI sentry somewhere in the lost wood.

And Woody knew he had failed the test, the true test of sacrifice. In his mind he heard the preacher from his church in Kilgore: "For whosoever will save his life shall lose it; and whosoever will lose his life for my sake shall find it. For what is a man profited if he shall gain the whole world and lose his own soul? Or what shall a man give in exchange for his soul?"

And in his drug-induced state, with his brain wrapped in tentacles that choked out the few remaining chances he had to redeem himself in this life, with whatever resolve he had left, Woody Wilson pledged to whatever gods there might be that his brothers in arms would not have died in vain, that he would never again fail the ultimate test. And when he finished this thought, he drifted even farther away to a place where there was only light, then only darkness.

EVEN THOUGH SHOT Glass called in the APB as soon as he got off the phone with Theodora Dixon, he waited in vain for any word about Schmutzer's Subaru.

"It's like he vanished into thin air," the dispatcher said.

Reynolds thought about it. "I'm afraid I have under-estimated Doc Smooth," Reynolds said. "He's crafty. He must have sensed we were on to him and switched cars. Since we didn't intercept him on the Interstate, he must have gotten off the highway right away. I'll have some guys start searching the area closest to the first few exits. We may get lucky and find the Subaru, which could lead us to him. Let me know if anybody reports a stolen car tonight."

"I'll keep you posted, Shot Glass," the dispatcher said.

"I hate to give Maggie this news," Reynolds said as he speed-dialed her on his cell.

Chapter 12

THE NEXT MORNING Waylon Wilson met Shot Glass Reynolds as he walked up the sidewalk of the precinct station house. He had a file folder in his hand. His eyes focused on some of the papers he had stuffed in it.

"Daddy never taught us about guns, Detective Reynolds," Waylon said. "So I wouldn't be much help to you in a fire fight. But I am one hell of a researcher."

"What you got?" Shot Glass asked him.

"I've done some background work on the Schmutzer place in Franklin."

"And?"

"And take a look at this," he said.

They barely made it in the door of the building before Waylon dumped the folder on the window ledge and pulled out some newspaper clippings.

"This one is from the Franklin paper just after the end of the war. It shows old man Schmutzer, Dr. Reinhold Schmutzer it calls him, with one of his sons. The son, it says, had come to visit to recuperate from injuries he suffered in Germany. Here's the picture Jessie found in a trunk in our attic that shows the man Daddy and Momma visited at the farm."

"Looks like the same guy all right," Reynolds said.

"And guess what?"

"What?"

"The article says the son, one Horatio Schmutzer, was a well-known psychiatrist who treated people for nervous breakdowns suffered as a result of battle fatigue," Waylon said. "It goes on to say that Reinhold's other son, Linus, was also a physician who remained in Germany to treat GIs in a military hospital."

"Have you found a member of the family that might be closer to my age?" Reynolds asked.

"I don't have a picture, but the birth records of Williamson county show a Linus Schmutzer, date of birth 5-10-58. The birth certificate lists Linus' father as Horatio."

"So the child was named after his uncle."

"Right. That child must be Doc Smooth," Waylon said. "The birth certificate indicates that the child's mother, June Riddlesbee of Franklin, died in childbirth."

Shot Glass put his right hand to his face, cupped his chin. "A child who never knew his mother," he said without further comment.

Waylon stopped for a minute and thought about Reynolds' remark. He continued as if he hadn't heard it. "I haven't turned up any records of the younger Linus' medical studies, licensure or anything like that. Momma said she met him hanging out around the marina in Panama City."

Reynolds interrupted him.

"I already called Panama City PD and had them go down to the marina and check it out. Everybody there knows and loves Mr. Woody, but no one ever heard of Doc Smooth, or Linus Schmutzer," Reynolds said.

Waylon processed this information for a minute. He took the index finger of his right hand and moved his rimless glasses further up on his nose.

"That doesn't make sense. Why would some guy pretend to have a boat at the marina and hang out with dad?"

"I don't know, but Panama City has no arrest record, nothing in the property tax records, no motor vehicle registrations, nothing," Shot Glass said. "Doc Smooth is a guy who doesn't want people to know anything about him."

"But it's pretty hard to fake an identity as a shrink," Waylon said.

"You would think," Reynolds said.

A thought struck Shot Glass.

"Come with me, Waylon," he said. "I just remembered something that might help."

They walked down the hall and sat down at the spare desk in the corner that Reynolds had dubbed his new office. He picked up the phone.

"Theodora?" he said as the receptionist answered.

"Detective Reynolds, I assume," she said.

"Doc Smooth gave us the slip yesterday," Reynolds said. "He must have figured out we were on to him."

"Oh, no," Ms. Dixon said. "So you haven't found your patient yet?"

"Not yet. You mentioned to me that Doc Smooth traded places with one of your regular doctors?"

"That's right."

"Can you give me the contact information for the facility where he went?"

"I'll get his file. Hold on a minute," Theodora said.

Reynolds listened to Barry Manilow for a couple of minutes while he was on hold.

Then she came back on the line.

"Our doctor is Richard Davis. The facility is listed as the Panhandle Mental Health Institute in Pensacola, Florida," she said. She gave him the number for the land line to the institute.

"The file doesn't have any personal contact information for Doctor Davis in Florida," she said after a minute.

"That seems strange," Reynolds said. "What if someone needed to reach him after hours to ask about one of his patients in Tennessee?"

"It does seem strange. Usually we have detailed contact information on all our doctors. We often have to call them about medication changes and stuff like that. I assumed that since Schmutzer took over his case load that he communicated with Doctor Davis as needed."

"Is there any information in the file on Doc Davis' family? An emergency contact or something like that?" Shot Glass asked.

"That stuff is usually contained in a sheet we attach to the inside front cover of the file. It looks like someone has removed it from Davis' folder," Dixon said.

"All right. Thanks again, Ms. Dixon."

"Let me know what else I can do, Shot Glass. This isn't sounding right to me," she said.

"Nor to me," Reynolds said as he hung up.

Waylon had been looking over Reynolds' shoulder as he took notes on his call with Theodora.

"If Doc Smooth worked at a place in Pensacola, why would he hang out at a marina in Panama City? That's at least a couple of hours drive one way," Waylon said.

"A lot of things aren't adding up," Reynolds said. He dialed the number for the institute in Pensacola. He put the phone on speaker so Waylon could hear.

"Mental Health Institute, how may I direct your call?" the receptionist said.

"This is Detective Reynolds with the Nashville, Tennessee, Police Department. I am trying to contact Dr. Richard Davis on urgent police business."

"I'm sorry, detective, but I am not familiar with a doctor by that name. Let me check with my supervisor for a minute." She put him on hold. In less than a minute another voice came on the line.

"Detective Reynolds? This is Mrs. Neal."

"Yes, ma'am."

"I'm the director of the administrative staff. We don't have a doctor by that name here," she said.

"The information I have indicates he is there on a sabbatical assignment in place of Dr. Linus Schmutzer, one of your staff psychiatrists," Reynolds said.

"Dr. Schmutzer was on staff here at one time, but he left several years ago. There is no Dr. Davis here on any sort of sabbatical," she said.

"Why did Schmutzer leave?" Reynolds asked.

"He was forced to resign," she said.

"What do you mean, Mrs. Neal?"

"The board of psychiatry permanently revoked his license to practice," she said.

"Why did the board do that, Ms. Neal?" Shot Glass asked.

"I can't tell you that, detective," she said.

"Mrs. Neal, we believe Dr. Schmutzer has kidnapped a man and is hiding him out somewhere. Time is of the essence. I can't stand on formalities here," Reynolds said.

"Was it an Alzheimer's patient he kidnapped?" she asked.

"Yes ma'am," Reynolds said. "Why do you ask?"

"He got his ticket punched for conducting unauthorized experiments on some of our patients with dementia. I hope you catch him soon," she said.

When Waylon heard Mrs. Neal's last comment, he slumped in his chair and put his face in his hands. Reynolds took the phone off speaker and picked up the handset.

"Thanks for your help, Mrs. Neal. Please give me a call if you think of anything else that might help."

"Good luck and Godspeed, Detective Reynolds," she said.

Chapter 13

AT HOME THAT evening in Bowling Green, Waylon sat on the couch. He muted the sound on the TV and glanced at the pictures that flashed across the screen as he gathered his thoughts in silence.

Jessie came over and sat down beside him, took his hand in hers.

"A penny for your thoughts," she said.

Waylon looked in her eyes and then dropped his gaze to their joined hands. He squeezed her hand before he spoke.

"It's not looking good for daddy," he began. "From what I learned today, I think the guy who grabbed him is an evil man with a history of abuse, or worse, towards Alzheimer's patients. I don't know what he would want with dad, but it can only spell trouble for him."

Jessie moved closer to Waylon, put her arm around his shoulder and hugged him. "He's going to be all right. I just know it," she said. "Woody has been a warrior all his life. He's got plenty of fight left in him," she said.

"I just hope it's enough," Waylon said. His eyes watered and he looked up at the TV screen, took a deep breath.

"The best we can tell, his kidnapper may have some ties to the Florida Panhandle. Momma said daddy had mentioned a character that visited him at the marina in Panama City from time to time. There is a psychiatrist named Schmutzer who came to a facility in Nashville ostensibly on some kind of sabbatical arrangement with another shrink from Pensacola. The administrator at the Pensacola facility didn't know anything about the swap and the doctor from Nashville never showed up there."

Waylon didn't share with Jessie what the administrator told Reynolds and him about Schmutzer's experiments on his patients with Alzheimer's.

"Detective Reynolds strikes me as the kind of man who will leave no stone unturned in his attempt to find daddy. I think I need to do what I can to help him," Waylon said. "That may mean that I'll be on the road for a while."

Jessie patted Waylon's knee.

"Woody raised a great son," she said. "You do what you have to do to bring your dad home safe. There's nothing in the world more important than that. I can manage things here for a while," she said.

"Thanks, baby," Waylon said. "I'll be thinking about you every moment I'm gone. I don't know how I ever got to be lucky enough to have you by my side."

"We're both awfully lucky," Jessie said. She hugged Waylon again and stood up. "I guess we had better get your bags packed."

"I guess so. It's a long drive to the Panhandle."

"That psychiatrist better watch his back. He doesn't know what he's up against with Detective Reynolds and Waylon Wilson on his trail," Jessie said.

"Damn straight," Waylon said as he hugged Jessie one more time for good measure.

Chapter 14

IT WAS NOT much after five o'clock when the summer sun rose out of the Gulf of Mexico and began to beat down on the sugar white sand of the Emerald Coast. A north wind pushed the waves back from the beach so that they died softly against the shore.

Woody Wilson awoke from his deep sleep, felt in the bed for Maggie and, when he didn't find her next to him, sat up. He didn't recognize the room, but had grown accustomed to the feeling that every day brought an unknown place, whether familiar or unfamiliar.

He got up, steadied himself against the foot of the bed, picked his wrinkled trousers off the floor and slipped into them. When he saw the beach out the window, he knew he was home, or close to home. He opened a sliding glass door that led onto a third floor gulf side balcony. He went to the railing and leaned over the side as far as he could. To the east, the coast nestled up to a string of high-rise condos in Panama City; to the west, the beaches of south Walton County jutted up against concrete tourist fortresses in San Destin.

He went back inside the multi-story house and entered the living area. With the shades drawn against the sun, the room was dark. He felt his way to an outside door, unlocked the deadbolt and darted out into the back yard. He turned a corner and headed straight for the water, his bare feet already aching to feel the sand between his toes, his eyes braced for the sting of the salt.

"I'm back, Maggie," he yelled at a couple of beachgoers who were taking a sunrise walk. They smiled as they saw the grin on his face, the childlike purity in his love of the moment. They scanned the beach for his partner, grew perplexed when they saw he was alone.

"Do you think he's all right?" the woman asked her husband.

"He's just having a good time," her husband said. "He's not bothering anyone."

His wife watched Woody as he ran all the way to the water and plunged into a wave. He swam a few yards out, then stood up and waded back to the shore.

"I guess you're right," she said.

"When I get to be his age, I hope people will leave me alone when I want to play in the water," her husband said. "It's a lot better than drooling on myself in a wheelchair at a nursing home."

His wife craned her neck over her shoulder as she continued to watch Woody.

"What if he's lost?" she said.

"Come on, baby," he said. "He's not our problem. He looks like he is perfectly capable of taking care of himself."

His wife took his hand in hers. Together they strolled along the beach, ever-distancing themselves from the inconvenient world of Woody Wilson, wrapped in the illusion that they could outlast the ineluctable waves of time, the hurricane of old age.

Chapter 15

DESPITE HER EIGHT-hour drive from Bowling Green to Seagrove Beach the day before, Maggie rose at five-thirty that morning, her internal clock forever set from forty-two years of school teaching.

With her coffee cup in hand, she walked out on the patio of the condo she and Woody had bought as their retirement home, a top floor, gulf front unit.

On the beach, she saw a man and woman in their mid-forties walking hand in hand as they enjoyed the sunrise, lost in each other, oblivious to the rest of the world.

Maggie remembered those days on the beach, the rhythm of the waves, holding Woody's hand or watching him skip rocks on the water, and she knew she had seen the last of them.

The time had come when if she were with Woody, she couldn't abandon her cares, cares for his well-being, his ability to squeeze out a few more days, or weeks, or months before the darkness took him away to a point beyond her reach.

It didn't matter to her. She just wanted him back with her until the end, his or hers.

She, too, unknown to Woody or Waylon, had spent a number of recent days in doctors' offices, subjecting herself to endless batteries of tests. Her soul, that part of her no test could measure, sensed something was wrong, wrong enough to make her worry if she could outlast Woody, if she could be there for him as long as he needed.

Her gaze drifted along the shoreline to the east and there, partially obscured by the high rise condo that jutted out towards the ocean, she caught a glimpse of a man in the water, an older man, bare-chested, wearing trousers and no shoes. She looked at him and squinted her eyes to focus on him. She hurried to the glass top table, grabbed the binoculars she used for dolphin watching and stuck them on her face. As she adjusted the lenses on the binoculars to sharpen her view, the man moved towards the dunes and the high rise blocked her view.

"It couldn't be," she said.

Maggie tossed the binoculars on the table, ran back inside the unit and threw on a swim suit cover-up. Outside she hit the button on the elevator, but when the door didn't open immediately, she turned and scampered down the four flights of stairs to the ground floor, jogged along the walkway towards the beach and hit the sand running.

When she reached the shoreline, she looked in the distance for the man she had seen, but he was gone. She ran east along the beach, wheezing from the effort, and approached the spot where she thought he should be.

The beach was vacant save for a few scavenging gulls

and a teenage boy setting out beach chairs for the occupants of the high rise.

Maggie went to the young man.

"Did you see an old man playing in the water out here a few minutes ago?" she asked.

The kid looked at the water where she pointed and thought about it.

"No, ma'am," he said. "I saw a couple of guys on the boardwalk a little while ago. But they were coming in, not going towards the water."

"Where did they go?" Maggie asked.

"Just up that way." He slung his left arm toward the boardwalk as he balanced six beach chairs on his shoulders.

"Was one of them an older man?" she asked.

"It looked like maybe an old dad and his middle-aged son," the boy said. "Kind of like when my dad hangs out with my grandpa."

Maggie ran towards the walkway, her feet slogged through the loose sand like car tires in thick mud. She was out of breath when she reached the top of the steps. She looked both directions and saw unit after unit, beach house after beach house. She knew the two men could be anywhere.

She slumped down on a bench seat built into the railing of the wooden walk and caught her breath. She felt around in her cover up and found her cell.

"Shot Glass," she said as the call went to voice mail. "Call me. I know where Woody is."

She hung up and rested long enough so she could get to her feet. Then she stood and limped back to her condo, ever-searching for some sign of Mr. Woody.

Chapter 16

"FROM NOW ON you need to tell me when you are leaving the house, Mr. Woody," Linus said when he got Woody back inside. "What if Maggie had come up while you were gone? She would have had my hide."

"Maggie?" Woody said. He looked around the room, trying to get his bearings. Finally he sat down in an overstuffed arm chair next to the couch.

"You said Maggie had gone to the store and would be back soon," Woody said. "She never came to check on me last night."

Linus moved next to an outside window and raised the edge of the shade. He could see Maggie sitting on the bench on the walkway, scanning the neighborhood, fear in her eyes, exhaustion showing on her face.

"I talked to her just a little while ago, Mr. Woody," he said as he positioned himself so that Woody could not see out the window. "She said she was at the Tom Thumb picking up some ice cream sandwiches."

Woody smiled for the first time in a couple of days. "She knows those are my favorite," he said.

"Why don't you see if you can rest for a minute until she gets here?" Linus said.

"All right. I am feeling a little tired after that swim," Woody said. He propped up his sandy feet on the hassock and laid his head on the back of the chair. In less than a minute, he began a faint snore, his breathing almost in tempo with the lapping waves of the unpredictable ocean.

Linus relaxed when he saw Woody drift off to sleep. Immediately he went into his bedroom and retrieved his medical bag from under the bed. He filled a syringe with a dose of medicine that would anesthetize Woody for the next twelve hours. When he started through the bedroom door towards the living room, Woody met him in the hallway.

He had a baseball bat in his hand, his eyes filled with rage, the skin tight across his face.

Linus tried to retreat into the bedroom and shut the door, but Woody was already on him.

"You're a liar, Doc Smooth. Maggie isn't coming," Woody said.

Schmutzer raised his right arm to deflect the blow as Woody swung the bat like a cleanup hitter in an all-star game. Linus fell backward and tried to catch himself, but Woody moved in and smacked him across the side of his head, the bat thumping like it had struck a watermelon and split it open. Schmutzer fell on the floor and he lay motionless, unconscious.

Woody stood over him a minute, then let the bat drop out of his hand. He knelt down and pried the syringe from Linus' fingers, held it up to the light.

"The medics gave me a lot of these shots when I was wounded in action in Germany," he said.

He stuck the needle in Linus' arm and pushed the plunger until all the medicine drained out.

"Sleep tight, Doc Smooth," he said as he closed the door to the bedroom.

Woody roamed through the house for several minutes, mad at the pictures on the wall, angry at the furniture. He grabbed a couple of tall bar stools and toppled them hard on the travertine floor. Finally he began to cool down.

He went into the room where he had slept and found his one small suitcase. He took out a clean change of clothes, went into the bathroom and took a shower.

"Got to be ready when I see Maggie," he said as he dabbed some cologne on his chest.

In the kitchen, he saw the keys to the Chrysler on the bar and stuck them in his pocket. He opened the door to Doc Smooth's bedroom and saw him still lying on the floor. He dragged and lifted him onto the bed, threw a blanket over him and turned out the light as he left.

When he got to the Chrysler, he placed his bag on the floor board within reach and started the car. It vibrated with the power of its big engine, straining to stretch its legs, to ramble along the narrow county road like a bull elephant defiantly warning the rest of the herd. Before he pushed the "D" button on the automatic transmission key pad Woody leaned down and felt around in his bag for something.

He recognized the cold steel and pulled out his 1911 Government Model Colt .45-caliber semi-automatic pistol. He released the magazine and checked to see that it was full, then jammed it in the handle of the gun, drew back the slide and chambered a round, put the hammer on half-cock. He placed the gun next to him on the seat and idled out the drive until he intersected County Road 30-A. He looked west about three hundred yards and saw cars streaming in and out of the twenty-four hour Tom Thumb convenience store, the only one within five miles. He pulled the car hard left and pushed the accelerator all the way to the floor.

"They're not going to get you, Maggie. I'm coming, sweetheart," he yelled as he closed on the store. He picked up the gun and prepared to engage the enemy.

Chapter 17

MAGGIE'S WALK BACK to the condo had taken almost an hour. She stopped every few minutes to catch her breath, feeling winded and nauseated from exertion.

She rode up the elevator slowly and sat down on an iron park bench in the exposed lobby outside her front door.

Her cell rang.

"Maggie. It's Shot Glass. I got your message. Where is he?"

"He's here," she said.

"Here as in Seagrove Beach?" Reynolds asked.

"Yes. I think I saw him on the beach a few hundred yards from our place, but when I went to find him, he was already gone," she said.

"Where are you now?" Reynolds said.

"I'm outside my condo. Why do you ask, Sherwood?"

"You might want to stand up and look over the railing at the parking lot."

Maggie got up slowly and peered down at the ground floor. Shot Glass leaned against his unmarked car and waved at her. In a second, Waylon moved away from the side of the building and stood next to Reynolds. He grinned at his momma.

"What on earth are you boys doing here?" Maggie yelled at them from the rail.

"We were just in the neighborhood and thought we would drop by to see you," Shot Glass yelled back at her.

"Well, get up here right now," Maggie said.

The men started towards the elevator.

"We better take the stairs," Waylon said. "That's the slowest and hottest elevator in Florida."

"Lead the way," Reynolds said.

Maggie met them at the top of the stairs. She grabbed Waylon and hugged him with both arms. She placed her head against his chest and closed her eyes. Then she hugged Shot Glass and patted him on the arm.

"Y'all are a sight for sore eyes," she said.

"How you doing, Momma?" Waylon asked. "You look like you might be a little out of breath."

"It's been a tough morning," Maggie said. "Let's go inside the condo where we can visit and I can sit in some air-conditioning."

Before Maggie could get her key in the door, they heard tires screech across the street at the convenience store. They looked in the direction of the noise and saw a large vintage car, blue and white, as it approached the store parking lot much too fast to make a turn. The passenger side front wheel of the car left the paved road and slammed down in a pothole. When the driver tried to pull the car back on the street, he caught the edge of a concrete abutment and blew out a tire.

The car began to skid sideways out of control until its driver's side front door slammed into the rear of a UPS truck third in line at the gas pump. Maggie, Waylon and Shot Glass could see the driver as the force of the impact pounded him against his door. The car horn began to sound as people in the parking lot responded to the crash.

A Walton County deputy on his coffee break at the Tom Thumb raced out the front door to the trapped driver who remained motionless in the front seat.

They heard the deputy call out to the man.

"Are you all right, sir? We'll get you out of there. Help is on the way," he said.

The deputy tried to pry the door open, but it was jammed from the force of the crash.

From their fourth floor perch, they saw the driver lay over on his side in the front seat, his head towards the passenger door.

The deputy ran to the other side of the car and yanked the door open. He began to reach in for the man, stopped and backed up, his hands held up in the air over his head.

Shot Glass, Maggie and Waylon watched as the driver crawled out of the car holding his left side with his left hand, a pistol with his right.

"Whoa," Shot Glass said. "It looks like that deputy could use some back up." He started for the stairs.

"Oh, no," Maggie screamed.

"What is it, Momma?" Waylon said.

"Look who it is," she said.

Waylon strained to get a good look at the driver as Reynolds stared at the scene.

"What is it?" Reynolds said.

"It's daddy," Waylon said as he wrapped his arms around himself and began to sob. "Please help him."

"I'm on my way. You and Maggie wait here," Reynolds said.

Shot Glass ran down the stairs and across the condo parking lot. He took a position next to a concrete wall that bordered the grounds of the complex, invisible as he approached the spot where Woody had the deputy cornered.

Reynolds had a clear view and a clear shot. He drew his Smith and Wesson .357-caliber revolver from his shoulder holster and held it in his right hand, pressed against his leg.

To the east on 30-A he could hear the wail of an ambulance's siren.

The EMTs stopped short of the Tom Thumb, but the emergency lights from their rescue vehicle strobed the scene like a disco dance floor.

Shot Glass could hear the deputy talking to Woody.

"Captain Woody. It's Jeff. Remember we talk about fishing all the time. I'm not here to hurt you."

Woody had a crazed look in his eyes; blood ran down the left side of his face from a cut sustained in the crash. He had his feet planted in a firing position, like a trained soldier, the gun pointed at Jeff's head, the hammer of the pistol fully cocked.

"Jeff?" Woody said. "Didn't we go out in the bay in the *Miss Maggie* one time?"

"Sure we did, Captain Woody. We caught a mess of speckled trout, and when we got back in, I cleaned 'em for you," Jeff said.

Woody thought about it for a minute. He lowered the gun just slightly.

"That was before you tried to hurt Maggie," Woody said as he raised the gun again. "If you want to keep breathing, you tell all these people to stand back while you take me inside to get her." Woody motioned with the gun toward the store. The young deputy waved the crowd back as he walked in front of Woody.

When Woody turned to follow Jeff inside, Reynolds had a shot. He braced his arm against a fence post, drew in a deep breath. He could feel the tension of the trigger against his right index finger.

Then he heard Maggie's screams.

"Woody. Woody. Woody," she yelled. She had made it to the heavy iron gate that blocked cars from entering the drive into the complex.

On her third cry, Woody stopped. He looked at the crowd, as he searched for a familiar face. He made a quarter turn of his body in the direction of the street.

"Woody. Woody. Woody," Maggie screamed again. She pounded the palms of her hands against the heavy gate, waved her arms in the air over her head.

Finally Woody focused on her.

"Maggie. Maggie," he said.

He let the gun drop to his side and ran towards her.

"Maggie. Maggie. Are you all right, baby?" he yelled at her.

Shot Glass saw a button that would open the gate and pressed it. As it swung open, Maggie ran towards Woody, her arms out-stretched.

Woody and Maggie met in the middle of County Road 30-A and grabbed each other as if they were bracing themselves against the winds of a tropical storm.

The gun dangled in Woody's right hand next to Maggie's back.

Shot Glass walked to the couple and took the gun away from Woody who offered no resistance. Reynolds slipped the magazine out of the pistol and ejected the live round from the firing chamber. He stood quietly, trying not to disturb them.

Woody and Maggie cried and kissed each other.

"I thought you were in trouble, baby," Woody said.

"I know, Woody," she said. "Thanks for rescuing me."

Deputy Jeff had approached Woody from behind.

"I need for you to hold your hands out in front of you, Captain Woody," he said.

Woody let go of Maggie and stretched both hands in front of him. Jeff put handcuffs on his wrists.

"We are going to take you to the hospital to get checked out, Captain Woody. Miss Maggie, you can ride with him In the ambulance," he said.

"Thank you, officer," Maggie said.

Waylon took Maggie's hand and walked her to the ambulance. The EMTs helped Woody and her up into the back of the vehicle. Waylon stepped in behind them.

"I'll catch up with you at the ER," Shot Glass said. Waylon nodded at him just before the EMTs closed the back door.

After the EMTs left, Reynolds walked over to the Walton County patrol car where Deputy Jeff sat in the driver's seat, the door opened. He had a Bic ball point pen with black ink in his hand. He was filling in a narrative of the events on the pre-printed lines of a standard police officer's offense report.

"Officer Jeff, I'm Shot Glass Reynolds, a detective with Nashville PD."

"Jeff Hansen," the deputy said.

They shook hands.

"You handled that situation well, Deputy Hansen," Reynolds said.

"Thanks, Detective. I was scared shitless."

"Me, too."

"You had a shot back there, didn't you?" the deputy looked at the location across the street where he knew Reynolds had positioned himself during the standoff.

"I did," Shot Glass said.

"Were you going to take it?"

"I was thinking about it."

Hansen nodded his head like he understood.

"This is a tough one. Everybody around here knows and loves Captain Woody. He didn't mean any harm. It's that damn Alzheimer's that took him over," Hansen said.

"What do you think will happen now?" Reynolds asked.

"The DA in this county is a real hard ass. I don't reckon he is going to take kindly to someone doing all this damage then pulling a gun on a uniformed law enforcement officer. My guess is that he will throw the book at him," Deputy Jeff said.

"Despite his disease?" Reynolds asked.

"The DA doesn't usually doesn't let niceties like that deter him much. Captain Woody dug a big hole for himself today. He'll have trouble climbing out."

"I reckon," Reynolds said. He shook hands with Hansen again and saluted him as he turned and walked across the parking lot.

He stopped next to a wrecker where the old Chrysler sat on the bed about to be towed. He flashed his badge at the tow truck driver.

"Can I look at the car for a minute before you leave," he said.

"It's a free country," the driver said.

"So they say," Shot Glass replied.

Reynolds circled the car, wrote down the plate number, looked at the underside of it.

"I make that a '56 Chrysler Imperial," he said after a while.

"That's what I would say," the tow truck driver said. "You don't see many of them on the road anymore. It's obviously been in storage and not around here, either."

"How do you figure that?" Reynolds asked.

"Cars don't last ten years in this salty environment. A fifty-year old beauty in this condition had to be stored in a controlled climate and babied for a long time," the wrecker driver said.

"So it probably belongs to a serious collector?" Reynolds asked.

"That'd be my guess."

"Mine, too. Thanks. I've got what I needed."

The driver got in his tow truck and pulled out on the road.

Shot Glass walked across the street to the condo complex and sat down in his car. He took his file on Woody from his briefcase and flipped through some pictures until he came to the one of Woody and Maggie at the farm in Tennessee where they visited Woody's friend. He got out his magnifying glass and focused on a section of the picture that caught the area between Woody's Corvette and the house. In the shade of a tree he saw the shadowy outline of another car.

"I'd say that's a new '56 Chrysler Imperial, if I were a betting man," he said as he closed the file and stuffed it back in his briefcase. He started the engine and drove out on County Road 30-A towards the hospital, where he planned to sit with Maggie, Waylon and Woody until the deputies took Woody to jail.

AS THE CROWD began to break up, a man wearing sunglasses and a straw hat with a broad brim that drooped down over the top part of his face lingered for a few seconds. He watched Reynolds' car until it was out of sight. He walked down the paved bike path to the east, his legs still wobbly from the after effects of the anesthetic, despite the antidote he had administered to himself.

When he came to his three-story beach house, he packed all his belongings and put them in the bed of a beat up Toyota truck. Then he went back in the house and wiped the place clean to eliminate any evidence, any tell-tale traces that he or Mr. Woody had ever been there. When he was satisfied with his work, he dead bolted all the doors and drove slowly, deliberately, out the drive until he came to County Road 30-A. At the stop sign, he paused for a minute as he considered his next move, then he turned right toward Panama City, to a special place where he knew Woody, or those who cared the most for him, would soon find themselves.

Doc Smooth would be there, too.

Chapter 18

PYTHAGORAS CLEMONS ROLLED out of bed, cleaned himself up and walked ten paces down the hall to his office. He plopped his wide seventy-eight year old ass down in the rolling chair behind his desk and surveyed the stacks of files that covered every square inch of the desk top. He tamped a Camel non-filtered cigarette from the package and lit the end of it with a wooden kitchen match. He smoked it down to a nub and crushed it out in the metal ashtray he hadn't emptied in two weeks.

He went into the kitchen and stared at the sink full of dirty dishes before he opened the fridge and pulled out a week old box of Krispy Kreme chocolate-covered old-fashioned donuts. He got the last two donuts out of the box and popped the first in his mouth, crunching on the dried sugar like a cow eating corn from a trough. He poured a cup of day old coffee in a left over McDonalds Styrofoam cup and stuck it in the microwave for forty-five seconds.

After he slugged down half the coffee, he grabbed his morning handful of pills and chugged them down with the dregs.

He walked out his front door, followed the driveway to the street and picked up the paper and checked the mail. He leafed through the stack of overdue bills and stuck them back in the mailbox.

He turned and looked at his yard where the weeds had choked the life out of any desirable plant. He went to the sign next to the driveway that read "Thag Clemons, Lawyer" and wiped a cobweb off it with the back of his hand.

He smoked another Camel in the front yard, threw it down on the gravel driveway, stomped it out and waved at his neighbor as he watered his roses.

"Go to hell, Clemons," the neighbor said just loud enough for Thag to hear it.

Thag acted like he hadn't heard the comment and trudged back to his porch where he sat on a swing that dangled on two chains attached to the ceiling. He rocked back and forth in the swing, his eyes closed. His beer belly stuck out of his unbuttoned shirt. He looked down at his dirty bare feet and wanted a drink of something stronger than day old coffee.

As he tried to get out of the swing, with a movement like a walrus wallowing on a rocky beach, he heard a car as it came up the drive. A man in his fifties wearing a windbreaker, khaki pants and a Polo golf shirt got out and walked towards him. He carried himself like a used up running back who had taken too many hits. When the man got to the porch, he sat down on a metal patio chair across from Thag and looked at him for a minute.

"Yeah?" Thag said.

"You Thag Clemons?"

"What's left of him."

"What kind of name is *Thag*?"

"Short for Pythagoras. My parents thought it was cute."

"You any good at math?"

"Not worth a damn," Thag said.

"Figures."

The two men looked at each other. The stranger rocked in his chair; Thag swayed back and forth on the side of the swing.

"I can figure well enough to tell you're a cop," Thag said.

The man placed his hands on the armrests of the patio chair and pushed himself up, moved closer to Thag and extended his hand.

"Shot Glass Reynolds, Detective Nashville, Tennessee, PD," he said. "You know Bum Wordsworth?"

"What's he done this time?" Thag asked.

"Nothing. I met him at the AA meeting last night. Afterwards, we rode over to a bar called The Dump," Reynolds said.

"I thought you had just been to an AA meeting?" Thag said.

"Bum said he wanted to have something new to confess at the next meeting," Reynolds said.

"Sounds like the Bum I know all right."

"There was a guy weighed about three hundred pounds tending bar. He had an Alabama T-shirt on, a long gray beard and bad teeth," Shot Glass said.

"That's Gorilla Hopkins. He's a mean sumbitch," Thag said.

Reynolds nodded.

"Well, I told Bum and Gorilla that I needed to find the

toughest yard dog criminal defense lawyer in Walton County," Reynolds said.

"And what'd they say?" Thag said.

"They said they didn't know anybody exactly like that, but they thought you were the next best thing," Reynolds said.

Thag shrugged his shoulders. "A man can't get no respect," he said.

"Tell me about it," Reynolds said. He moved another step closer to Clemons, looked him in the eye.

"I have a potential client for you. He's in jail. The charge is attempted capital murder of a police officer," Reynolds said.

"Shit. That's an automatic life sentence. Why would a cop want to help a guy charged with almost killing a cop?"

"He reminds me of my dad. I like his wife. I'm a nice guy," Reynolds said. He spoke in a clipped staccato, like short bursts of machine gun fire. "And he has Alzheimer's. He had just escaped from his kidnapper, and he was out of his head at the time of the attack."

Thag put his feet on the floor of the porch, steadied himself and headed towards the door.

"Come on in," he said as he held the door open for Shot Glass.

Inside Reynolds stepped over old newspapers and around piles of books as he followed Clemons to his office. Clemons cleared a spot for him in a straight backed chair. He dropped issues of the *New York Times* on the floor next to Reynolds' feet.

"Nice place," Reynolds said.

"I haven't done much housekeeping since my wife passed away," Clemons said.

"When was that?"

"It'll be sixteen years the seventeenth of next month."

"Looks about right," Reynolds said.

Clemons took a yellow legal pad and flipped to an empty page. He asked Reynolds about the case. Reynolds gave him the twenty-five words or less version. Clemons took down a few notes, put his pen down.

"The DA here is an asshole. Actually it's worse than that. He's a thirty-five-year-old prick who inherited the job after his prince of a dad went on to glory. He's a pure political operative who sits on the front pew at church on Sunday and screws poor sumbitches who don't deserve it the rest of the week. He won't listen to reason about anything, but especially about something like this that will make good press for him."

"So I heard."

"I'll go talk to him, but I expect he will tell me to go screw myself."

Clemons buttoned his shirt so that it covered his paunch.

"What would Wilson's wife like to see happen to Woody?" he asked.

"She wants him home," Reynolds said.

"Is she able to take care of him? An Alzheimer's patient is a handful," Clemons said.

"She thinks she can. I have my doubts. She loves him too much to watch him waste away," Shot Glass said.

Clemons picked up a pair of reading glasses with half lenses and twirled them around as he held them between the thumb and index finger of his left hand. He looked out the office window at his neighbor's manicured back yard. In a minute he laid the glasses down and looked at his hands. He studied the age spots for a minute like he thought they might go away if he inspected them one by one.

Then he looked Reynolds in the eye.

"I'll be seventy-nine years old on my next birthday, Reynolds. I've seen too much already. You know those guys who go around and preach about intelligent design?"

"Yeah, I've heard a few of them," Reynolds said.

"They haven't spent much time around people with Alzheimer's," Clemons said.

"No, sir. They haven't."

Thag wallowed in the hopelessness for a minute before he spoke again.

"I don't suppose any of Woody's loved ones have the resources necessary to fund the defense of a case like this," Clemons said.

"Woody and Maggie bought a place on the Gulf many years ago. She's a retired teacher. He worked for the post office. I'm sure they have some savings," Reynolds lied.

"Are you on the clock?"

"I told Maggie I'd help her find Woody. Now he's found, but I can't drop out on her. I'm in for the duration."

"What does your captain think about you being on the road for a while?"

"I came down here as part of an official assignment to lead an investigation. I was ordered to find Woody, rescue him and nab his kidnapper. I am still working on the rescuing and nabbing part of the assignment. I figure the chief will give me a little time to keep looking for Doc Smooth, but it would be nice if you could see that Woody beats the rap in the meantime."

"You're saying it doesn't help you much if your kidnap victim gets convicted of trying to kill a cop?"

"Something like that."

"So you are asking me to jump into the defense of a high

profile case, with inadequate financial resources, push it on the fast track to trial, work night and day for weeks and do it all for free?"

"Something like that."

Clemons allowed a grin to creep on his face. It looked like it would gouge crevasses in the yellowed skin that stretched taut across his forehead.

"You know what lawyers call working for free?"

"Pro bono?"

"Bad judgment."

He walked around his desk and shook hands with Shot Glass. "Count me in," Clemons said as he winked at him.

Clemons noticed Reynolds' eyes had a faint mist.

"I'll drop by the jail in the next day or so and introduce myself to Woody. Why don't you bring Maggie by here in the morning around ten o'clock so we can get acquainted?"

"Maybe it would be better if you came by her place," Reynolds said as he scanned the piles on the floor, the stacks on the furniture, the trash cans jammed to overflowing with old fried chicken boxes.

"Okay. I can take a hint. Tell her to expect me around ten o'clock."

"Thanks, Thag. I know it will mean a lot to her."

"Let's just hope I can do Woody some good."

Reynolds got up and let himself out of the house as Clemons jotted down a few more notes on his yellow pad.

When Thag saw Reynolds' car pull out of the drive, he opened the liquor cabinet behind his desk and filled a shot glass with the last drops from a bottle of single malt scotch. He swirled it under his nose for a minute and savored the heavy scent, raised it to eye level.

"To Woody, Maggie and Shot Glass Reynolds," he said. Then he threw the whiskey into the back of his throat. His head snapped back as the amber liquid burned its way to his stomach.

Chapter 19

AT THE ER, the doctors put five stitches above Woody's left eye and wrapped his rib cage with a cloth band to stabilize three cracked ribs on the left side. They gave him two sample bottles of hydrocodone tablets with instructions to take one or two every four hours as needed for pain.

The deputies let Maggie ride in the back seat of the patrol car with him to the jail but refused to let her in the booking room where they finger printed him and took his mug shot. When they finished booking him in, they brought him to a visitation cell where a thick, bullet proof plate glass window separated them.

Maggie picked up the phone handset and waved it at Woody so he would know to pick up the one inside his cage.

"They are going to let you visit with some guys here for a little while, Woody," she said. "I'll be back to see you in the morning."

"Do you have to go, baby?" Woody said.

He was on the verge of tears.

"It's the way they do it. It's just like you're back in basic training. They make the rules; you follow them. I'll have you out of here before you know it, hon. Promise me you'll be on your best behavior, so they will let you out sooner," Maggie said.

"I'll be a model GI," Woody said as he saluted her, got up and knocked on the heavy steel door behind him. He waved at her on his way out the door.

Maggie sat in the room for a couple of minutes, trying to compose herself, to sort things out. Then she took a handkerchief from her purse, wiped her eyes, threw her head back and marched out into the jail lobby like a commander inspecting his troops.

They took Woody to a barracks type cell that housed nine prisoners including him. A twenty-year-old white kid with scraggly brown hair, arms covered in tattoos, and bad teeth from meth abuse pointed at a top bunk.

"That one's for you, grandpa," he said as he laughed and grinned at his other bunkmates.

Woody walked over to him and looked at the inked writing on his right forearm.

"Were you in Auschwitz?" he asked him.

The young boy backed away from Woody about half a step.

"Auschwitz? What the hell is that?"

"A concentration camp in Poland. My unit was the first one in there," Woody said. "I had a good friend who survived it, but he is dead now."

"No, man. These are just tattoos I got for show. The chicks love that shit. Know what I mean?" He elbowed Woody.

Woody looked at him like he was from another planet.

"The Germans tattooed the prisoners' identification numbers on their arms. It wasn't for show," Woody said.

The young man folded his arms and placed the palms of his hands on the soft skin of the underside of his forearms to hide the tattoos. When he saw no one was laughing, he climbed up into one of the top bunks, covered himself with a gray wool blanket frayed around the seams and turned his head to the wall.

Woody looked around the room at the other inmates.

"My friend usually wore long sleeve shirts after the war. It was the fashion in those days. Sometimes he rolled his sleeves far enough back so that he could see the identification number and remember what the concentration camp was like."

A black guy about twice Woody's size came and stood next to him. He had a front tooth missing from a recent bar fight, his head shaved so that the light of the bare bulb that dangled overhead reflected off it.

"My father fought in the European theater, too," he said. His diction was precise, like a World War Two scholar delivering a lecture. "He told me he saw bodies stacked up like firewood at those camps."

Woody looked at the black man and nodded. "I can't talk about that yet," he said. "What's your dad's name?"

The black man looked at Woody. He thought about the stories his father had told of combat, of brotherhood forged in the fire of death among people who would never have known each other in the peacetime world.

"Odessa Sheffield. He was one of the guys who removed mines from the roads. He told me he crawled on his belly for hundreds of yards at a time with nothing but a field knife in his hand, praying that he didn't trip one of those sumbitches. He made it home but died a few years ago in a car wreck when one of Francis' friends hopped up on dope crossed the median on the Interstate and hit him head on."

"Francis?" Woody asked.

The black man looked up at the back of the tattooed boy who had tried to give Woody grief.

"My folks are coonasses. They didn't know any better," Francis said as he spoke to the wall without turning to face Woody and the black man.

"His full name is Theophilus Francis," the black man said.

Woody thought about the kid's name for a minute.

"Theo Francis? Your folks weren't kin to Johnny Cash, were they kid?" he asked and waited for his words to sink in. "You know, a boy named Sue?"

The men heard Francis as he stifled a laugh.

"Not that I know of, grandpa," he said to the wall.

Woody thought about the name of the black man's father.

"Odessa Sheffield. Was he a tall skinny guy with gold caps on his two front teeth and wavy black hair, a guy who walked like he had a cob up his ass and quoted passages from the Sermon on the Mount?" Woody asked.

The inmate froze.

"What did you ever hear this guy say?"

"He loved to quote the Beatitudes. That's what Bro. Bruce called those sayings right after the begats in the book of Matthew. 'Blessed are the peacemakers, for they shall be called the children of God,' he would say. I used to tell him it was crazy for a foot soldier to say stuff like that. He would smile and tell me that whatever Jesus said was all that really mattered. 'Hide and watch. You'll see how it all comes out in the end,' he'd say," Woody said.

"I heard him say that a thousand times when I was growing up," the inmate said. "My name is Odessa Sheffield, Jr." He stuck out his hand and Woody shook it like a cowboy pumps a well handle to get a trickle of water from the spigot on a hot summer day.

"It's my great pleasure to meet you, Mr. Sheffield. My name is Woodrow Wilson, but you can call me Woody."

"Everyone 'round here just calls me Odd. You might as well join the crowd."

Odd Sheffield motioned for Woody to take a seat on one of the bottom bunks. "You can have this one," he said. "I was ready to move upstairs anyway."

Woody sat on the bunk and leaned his face forward into his hands. He grabbed his left side and winced when pain from his ribcage shot through him. Sheffield helped him lie down on the bed, gave him the pillow off his bunk.

"Hold this tight against you and it will help the pain, sir," he said. "I've had some broke ribs. They're a bitch."

"You ain't a kidding. Thank you, Odd," Woody said as he closed his eyes.

The black man stared around the room at the other inmates until they returned to their usual routines as if Woody had never joined them.

"I did my time in Vietnam. You can think what you want about me, but this man is worthy of our respect," Sheffield said.

Chapter 20

WHEN WOODY HAD been in jail three days, Waylon Wilson drove to Pensacola and talked to the staff at the Panhandle Mental Health Institute. After three hours of interviews, he came up with exactly one lead on the possible whereabouts of Linus Schmutzer II. He started to call Shot Glass but decided it was time he graduated to some independent investigative work.

He crossed Pensacola Bay and drove east on Highway 98 through Navarre Beach and past Eglin Air Force base. On the west side of Ft. Walton, he turned into a driveway that led to a house that bordered the Gulf Intracoastal Waterway. There was a for sale sign in the front yard. Waylon had called the realtor pretending he was an interested buyer and gotten the code for the lock box.

The power to the house was off and the darkness inside seemed inconsistent with the oppressive, humid heat that permeated the residence.

Waylon walked to the large plate glass window in the living area that overlooked the water and drew the curtains back.

A power boat with a lone fisherman tucked under the slight shade of a T-top cut through the water near shore and bounced over the two-foot waves on its way to the hungry redfish in Choctawhatchee Bay. The captain saw Waylon throw the shades open and waved as if he knew the usual inhabitant of the place. Waylon waved back and watched the boat until it was out of sight.

Waylon forgot about his mission and let his mind drift to an earlier time, a time when once he and his dad took their twenty-eight foot Parker boat out for a six day cruise of the Gulf Intracoastal Waterway. They came out of St. Andrew Bay and ran to Apalachicola, Woody the captain and Waylon his first mate. The first night they encountered a sudden storm and ran to cover. Waylon thought he was a goner.

Woody just laughed and sang and said, "The *Miss Maggie* ain't scared of a little squall like this, son. But there is something you always need to remember in a situation like this."

"What's that, daddy?" Waylon asked as he clung to the steel rail on the side of the cabin with both hands.

"Red, right, return." Woody pointed at the lights that marked the channel ahead of them. Waylon could see a string of red ones.

"When you are going out to sea, the red lights are on your left. But if you're trying to get home to port, keep them on your right and you'll be all right."

"Yes, sir," Waylon told his dad.

And sure enough they were all right. They made it

safely to a spot along a tributary where they got out of the wind and spent the night on the deck eating mullet they caught after they dropped anchor.

Woody got out his harmonica and played as Waylon sang "The Red River Valley" and "Tumbling Tumbleweeds," their favorite songs.

The next morning Woody found some oyster beds, and they harvested a bushel sack full of oysters and put them on ice 'til sundown when they shucked and ate half of them. They dipped them in homemade cocktail sauce and Tabasco and squirted lemon juice on them.

All these years later, Waylon could feel the fresh oysters as they slithered down his throat and the hot sauce burned his lips.

During the day they fished for speckled trout and red drum. Once they found a deep hole, and Woody showed Waylon how to use a big artificial lure to draw a gag grouper out of its safe spot. Waylon fought it twenty minutes before he got it aboard. Woody hugged his neck and put the fish on ice.

"We got to get a picture of that one before we eat it," he told Waylon. And the next day when another boat passed them, Woody hailed the captain and had him tie on to the *Miss Maggie.* The other skipper had his son with him, too.

Woody handed the captain his camera and took his place next to Waylon while he snapped the picture. Waylon remembered how his arm ached as he held the ten-pounder as high as he could reach.

Woody gave the skipper of the boat the rest of the oysters and promised to send him a copy of the picture when he got it developed. Waylon and the captain's son saluted each other like Navy seamen when the boats began to drift apart.

Two weeks later when he got the prints back from the photo shop, Woody asked the man at the counter to make two eight-by-tens of the shot of him standing next to Waylon, grinning as Waylon strained to hold the fish shoulder high. He bought a frame for one of the pictures and put the other in a large manila mailer and sent it special delivery to the address the other captain had given him. He hand wrote a note to the sailor and hung the framed picture over his desk at the post office, where it remained until he retired twenty years later.

Waylon walked down to the sea wall, stood among the sea oats, smelled the salt water. He found a smooth stone near the water and skipped it hard against the bay. He watched as it bounced a half dozen times before it sank to the silt-covered bottom never to be seen again.

Then he thought of a conversation Woody had with him the night before he left for college to study computers.

"You can study what you want, Waylon. But I'd love to see you take my place at the post office one day," he said. "This computer business is never going to pay anything."

Waylon knew his dad was old-fashioned, a pencil and Big Chief tablet kind of man, who didn't use a calculator to figure postage if he could avoid it. He thought the measure of a man was what he could do from within himself, without resorting to artificial aids that did the work for him. But he didn't hold Waylon back and was the proudest dad in the crowd when Waylon graduated *summa cum laude* from The University of Texas and landed an IT job when they were few and far between.

From that day forward, Woody bragged to his buddies about his son, the computer genius.

Waylon turned to walk back towards the house and

stumbled on a spot of uneven ground where a mound half-covered in a new growth of grass protruded a few inches above the rest of the yard. When he caught his balance, he knelt down and examined the dirt. It was a couple of feet across and about six feet long. Waylon looked a few feet beyond the edge of the mound and saw another one, still bare and muddy.

They looked like graves.

He scanned the yard, sprang to his feet and ran toward his car. He glanced over his shoulder at the house and strained to see anyone who might be watching him from a curtained window.

He reached his car and threw it in gear, did a donut in the yard and hurdled out the drive on to Highway 98. When he was out of sight of the house, he turned down a side street into a residential area north of the highway away from the water and parked under a branch of an oak that shaded the road.

He took out his cell.

"Shot Glass, you better get down here. I think I have found something at Doc Smooth's house," he said as he ended the call.

Chapter 21

THAG KNOCKED ON Maggie's door the next morning at ten o'clock sharp. In less than thirty seconds she answered.

"Thag Clemons," he said as he stuck out his hand.

"Sherwood told me you were coming, Mr. Clemons," Maggie said as she took his hand. "I have some coffee and cookies if you'd like."

"I never turn down coffee and cookies," Thag said as he glanced at his stomach that bulged against the bottom two buttons of his shirt.

He followed Maggie down the travertine hallway to the living room that did double duty as a dining area. He put three sugar cookies on a small Styrofoam plate and poured himself a cup of coffee from a thermos. The hot liquid steamed in his cup.

He laid a file folder on the six foot pine table and waited for Maggie to take a seat opposite him. When she had arranged herself, he started in.

"Detective Reynolds briefed me on the facts, but I need to get a feel for Woody. Every case is more about the person than the facts in my experience. I have a pretty good idea that Woody's story is something out of the ordinary and that you are the only person in the world who really knows him from the inside out." He stopped and watched Maggie's face for a minute. She had never taken her eyes off him as he spoke. He felt like she could see clear through him.

"You and I are too old to beat around the bush with each other, Mr. Clemons," Maggie began.

"Woody Wilson is the greatest person I have ever known. As Jesus said about one of his disciples, he is a man in whom there is no guile."

Thag wished the same could be said of him. And he wished a woman like Maggie Wilson would say it. A man could do a lot worse he thought.

"Woody grew up a country boy in East Texas, went off to fight World War Two and came home to help build a world worth what he had endured in Germany. The best I can tell, he did a good job of it," Maggie said. She held a plastic fork in her hands as she talked, examined the tines one by one before she continued.

"He witnessed unspeakable horrors in the war, horrors no person should encounter, yet alone a gentle soul like Woody. He is a kind, loving man who would give you the shirt off his back. He found himself in the killing fields and did his duty. It damaged his spirit somehow, but he held it all inside until Alzheimer's brought it out in the open."

Thag doodled on a yellow legal pad while she talked. When she finished, he put his pen down and laid his hands face down on the table.

"When did you first recognize the dementia, Mrs. Wilson?"

"Three or four years ago, he started to repeat himself, to lose track of simple things, forget something he had already done, like taking out the trash. Soon he began to alter his daily routine, to stay at home more, spend less time joy-riding up and down the beach road. He had always been fastidious in his grooming. Then he began to go several days without shaving or taking a shower.

"Woody met his coffee-drinking buddies at the Wheelhouse Café down the street weekday mornings at six o'clock. One morning around nine his buddy, Carruthers, called to tell me Woody hadn't arrived at the meeting, but that they had seen him driving up and down the road like he was looking for something. About ten-thirty that morning, I heard Woody come in. He was trembling and on the verge of tears. He told me the guys had moved the meeting without telling him. He got agitated and started searching for his pistol. I didn't tell him Carruthers had called. In a few minutes, he calmed down and forgot all about it.

"The next morning, I got up with him and drove him to the Wheelhouse. I sat in a corner out of the way while his friends and he held court. Woody was happy as a lark."

"Did he ever threaten you, Mrs. Wilson?" Thag asked.

"Never. Not in a million years," she said. "All he's ever wanted to do was protect me."

Maggie could not hold back her tears. She sobbed as she buried her face in her handkerchief, embarrassed to make such a display in front of Thag.

Thag got up and walked to the counter where he plucked a handful of tissues from a Kleenex box. The box had a blue ocean print on the side. He laid the tissues in front of

Maggie and touched her arm before he took his seat across from her again.

"I don't want to open old wounds, Mrs. Wilson, but I think you need to understand how this case will play out," Thag said. "In cases like this, I have to decide if I will ask the judge to appoint a psychiatrist to examine Mr. Wilson to determine if he is competent to stand trial. If I play that card, Mr. Wilson's fate will be in the hands of the psychiatrist. If the psychiatrist finds that Mr. Wilson is not competent to stand trial, then the judge will send him to a psychiatric ward to remain until such time as he regains competence, if ever. If the shrink finds he is competent, then Woody will go to trial just like anyone else charged with this crime would."

Thag paused for a minute to let his words sink in.

"You're telling me Woody could be in a mental hospital for the rest of his life if the psychiatrist finds him incompetent?" Maggie asked.

"Yes, ma'am. Although in my experience the state wouldn't want to pay the bill for such services indefinitely. At some point, he might be released into your custody."

"What if he finds him competent to stand trial and he goes to court?"

"If he is found guilty of the charge, it's an automatic life sentence in this state. He would go to the penitentiary with no hope for parole. Of course, if a jury finds him not guilty, he is a free man."

Maggie thought about the options.

"Well, Woody did point a gun at the deputy. Those facts are clear. I would imagine any DA worth his salt would have little difficulty turning that fact into enough to convict."

"You're probably right about that, Mrs. Wilson," Thag

said. "Our only hope in that situation would be if the jury identified with your husband and his plight and decided to disregard the law and let him go free."

"What are the odds on that?"

"You can never tell what a jury will do. I figure we have a better chance than usual of something like that happening because Mr. Wilson is such an extraordinary and likable person. But I still guess it's about a two-to-one chance the jury would convict," Thag said. He saw no reason to sugar coat it. Not with someone like Maggie Wilson.

"Probably more like five to one," Maggie said.

Thag nodded his head like a kid caught cheating.

"So our best hope is that the psychiatrist finds him not competent to stand trial," Maggie said. "How often does that happen?"

"I've seen it once in fifty years," Thag said. "But it's the best chance we have."

He stuffed his last cookie in his mouth, washed it down with the rest of the coffee in his cup, pushed his chair away from the table and stood up.

Maggie walked him to the door. When they got to the foyer, she picked up an envelope from a wooden bench and gave it to Thag.

"What's this?" Thag said.

"Your retainer."

"I don't require a retainer in this matter, Mrs. Wilson. Shot Glass enlisted me as a foot soldier. I am proud to be of service in any way I can. We have an uphill battle."

"I know, Mr. Clemons. Shot Glass has his heart in the right place and so do you. But I don't expect you to work for free. Woody always says that a day's work is worth a day's pay." She pressed the envelope in his hand and wouldn't take it back.

"Well, then thanks, Mrs. Wilson," Thag said.

"You can call me Maggie, if I can call you Thag," she said.

"Yes, ma'am, Maggie." Thag stuck the envelope in his pocket, walked out the door, took the elevator to the ground floor.

He drove his Toyota across the street to the Tom Thumb and pulled up next to a gas pump. While he filled his tank, he took the envelope out of his pocket. He tore the seal lose with his thumb and saw a check inside. He started to tear up the envelope and throw it in the trash, then he thought about the clump of bills stuck in his mailbox at the house. He pulled the check out of the envelope.

It was for ten thousand dollars.

He folded it and stuck it in his pocket before the woman next to him pumping gas could see it.

Chapter 22

THAG HAD MET a lot of prisoners in his day: young men who ruined their lives in search of a fix, middle-aged losers who beat their wives because they couldn't face another stretch of time without lashing out at someone incapable of self-defense, old winos who sold their souls for a cheap bottle of Mad Dog 20-20. But he had never sat in an interview room with a man like Woody Wilson.

A guard brought Woody to the holding cell. Woody shook his hand and slapped him on the back when the guard took his key and unlocked his handcuffs.

"Let me know when you're ready to come back into the cell block, Mr. Woody," the guard said.

"Ten-four, Bartholomew," Woody said to the guard as he watched him lock the heavy iron door behind him.

"He has a new baby on the way any day now," Woody said to Thag as he motioned towards the hallway where the guard had been.

"Good for him," Thag said. "I remember those nights when we brought our new son home from the hospital. We counted the days until he slept all night."

"Yeah. Waylon, that's my boy, didn't sleep all night for two months. I thought Maggie and me were never going to get a good night's sleep again," Woody said. His eyes twinkled as he chuckled.

"That was a long time ago," Thag said.

"A life time," Woody said.

Thag looked at his intake questionnaire that lay on the table.

He had written 'Woody Wilson' in the first block; 'attempted capital murder of a police officer' in the second.

"My name is Pythagoras Clemons," he said. "I'm your lawyer."

"Do I need one?" Woody asked.

"I reckon so, Mr. Wilson. You're facing an automatic life sentence because of the incident at the Tom Thumb."

IN THOSE BRIEF moments Woody had drifted away. The fighting at the Battle of the Bulge was over. The soldiers were resting, whoring, trying to forget as best they could the events of the last five weeks. He had left them to search the woods for a deer he had seen, an old-timer with a twelve-point rack. Mid-morning he spotted the buck on the edge of a secluded wood and took dead aim. But when he had him in his sights, he relaxed his finger on the trigger of his rifle.

"I'm through with killing," he said under his breath as he watched the grand buck stroll off into the shelter of the dense forest. Woody walked to the center of a clearing where a massive oak lay on its side. He sat down on the toppled trunk

ridden with bullet holes and laid his rifle across his knees. Just then a German girl appeared in the wood. She looked about fifteen years old, her face painted pink with diluted rouge, her ragged clothes draped lose on her bony skeleton, her hair cropped short in a self-inflicted coiffure. She crossed the open area and sat on the other end of the fallen tree, almost close enough for Woody to touch her. She smiled at him and unbuttoned her blouse. Woody could see her bare breasts.

He got up and ran into the woods, his rifle in his right hand, his thoughts back home.

HE SNAPPED BACK to the jail cell.

"My dad would have whipped me within an inch of my life with a cane pole if I had laid a hand on that girl," he said to Thag. "It wouldn't a mattered a bit to him that the other guys were doing stuff like that. 'You have to be your own man' he would have said as he gave me what for. And he would have been right, too."

Thag tried to catch the thread.

"What girl?"

"A girl I knew for a minute or two in Germany about sixty-five years ago. She comes to see me now and then when I least expect her. I've often wondered if some other GI rescued her from that hell hole and brought her home with him. She couldn't hold a candle to Maggie."

"It was Maggie who sent me to see you, Mr. Wilson," Thag said.

"You've seen her?"

"Yes, sir. I saw her yesterday morning at your condo."

"When is she coming to visit me?"

"She comes every day."

Woody erupted, pounded the metal table with his fist, pushed his folding chair away from it.

"Is she here now? I need to see her." He got up and went to the thick glass window of the holding cell, craned his neck to see around the corner, scanned for any sign of Maggie.

"Have a seat, Mr. Wilson. She'll be along after we finish our visit."

Woody sat down again, calm now. He looked at Thag.

"Who did you say you were, sir?"

"I'm your lawyer, Pythagoras Clemons, Mr. Wilson."

"Oh, yeah. The deal at the Tom Thumb. I was afraid they had Maggie and were about to hurt her. I couldn't let that happen. I didn't shoot anybody, did I?"

"No, but you scared the shit out of a deputy sheriff."

Woody laughed. "He probably had it coming," he said. "Which one was it?"

Thag looked at his notes. "A young guy named Hansen."

"Hansen? I remember him. He went fishing with me one time. We caught red snapper, and he cleaned 'em for me. He's a nice kid. I'm sorry he's the one I jumped. Is he okay?"

"I think he's fine, Mr. Wilson."

Woody interrupted him. "Mr. Wilson was my dad. I'm Woody."

"All right, Woody. I'm Thag."

"Thag. I like having a lawyer named Thag. We'll make a good team, I bet, Thag."

"We're the A-team, Woody."

"Damn straight. What do we do now?" Woody asked.

"The most important thing is that we become friends. I'll be spending a lot of time with you and I need you to shoot straight with me."

"I always tell the truth, Thag. Problem these days is that I can't remember much. When something comes to me I try to hold on to it, but it slips away before I can grab onto it. I'll do the best I can."

"That's all I can ask of you. I'll do the same."

"I like you, Thag. Thanks for coming to see me," Woody said. He got up and walked to the heavy iron door, banged the palm of his hand against it until he saw Deputy Bartholomew wave at him from the observation desk.

"We're not done yet, Woody," Thag said. "We have a lot of ground to cover."

"I'll see you later this afternoon, Thag. Right now I have to get cleaned up before Maggie gets here."

Deputy Bartholomew opened the door, stepped in and put Woody's handcuffs on.

"That new baby boy come yet, Bart?" he asked the jailer.

"Not yet, Mr. Woody. Anytime now."

"Tell the missus I'm praying for her," Woody said.

The jailer turned Woody toward the door, patted him a couple of times on his shoulder with his right hand and left his hand on his shoulder as he guided him down the hall until they turned a corner and Thag lost sight of them both.

Pythagoras Clemons put his papers in his briefcase, latched it closed and sat at the K-mart aluminum table for a long time.

"Woody Wilson deserves a lot better than me," he said. Then he got up and punched a call button. In a minute he heard the door latch click behind him and he pushed the door open and walked out into the waiting room. He waded through a pool of pimps and bail bondsmen, rode the elevator to the ground floor. When he got to the outside steps of the courthouse, he dropped his valise on the sidewalk, took out a Camel and had a smoke.

As he made his way to his car, he offered up a short prayer, the first he had uttered since his wife's passing. He prayed for Deputy Bart's wife, his unborn son, Woody Wilson, and his own sorry ass.

Chapter 23

THE NEXT DAY Thag Clemons parked his 1995 Toyota Corolla in the Walton County employee parking lot in a spot reserved for law enforcement personnel. He reached into the glove box and grabbed a handicapped sticker and hung it like a coat hanger on the rear view mirror. He bumped his hip against the driver's door to make the door latch and left the car unlocked with the windows rolled down.

He walked across the marble floor of the lobby and rode the elevator to the fourth story where he dropped his briefcase next to the receptionist's desk. He pulled a handkerchief from his coat pocket and wiped the sweat off his face.

"Is he in?" he asked the stern lady who acted as the gatekeeper for the DA's office. She was about forty-five years old, dark hair. A pair of black horn rim glasses dangled from her neck on a faux silver chain. Behind her on the desk was a high school graduation picture of her daughter and a coffee cup with the words "First Baptist Women of God" stenciled on it in black letters.

"He who?" she said.

"He, the man. Who else?" Thag replied.

"Do you mean Mr. Rudd Brightwell?"

"I mean Mr. Rudd Brightwell, Jr., the people's champion," Thag said.

"Who might I say is here to see him?"

Thag looked at her for a minute, then surveyed the room where staff people and assistant DAs he had known for twenty years milled around without giving him the time of day. He reached into his shirt pocket and drew out a business card. It had an old address marked out with pencil. Above it he had interlineated his home address.

"Thag?" she said. "What kind of name is that for a lawyer?"

"The kind that makes you watch your back," he said.

She laid the card on her desk and moved a few sheets of paper around. She checked the extension numbers on a list in front of her and dialed one.

"Jewel, there's a guy named Fig Clemons here who wants to see the district attorney."

She looked up at Thag while she waited for an answer. Thag couldn't make out the voice on the other end of the call. The receptionist nodded into the phone without speaking and motioned at a row of chairs that backed up against the gray carpeted wall.

"Take a seat," she said.

After he waited fifteen minutes, Thag saw a woman in her mid-sixties with gray hair pulled up into a bun approach him from a long corridor that ran back through the maze of worn and battered metal desks in the government office anteroom.

"It's been a while," Jewel said.

Thag stood and took her hand. "It's always a pleasure, Jewel."

She punched him on the shoulder and turned to walk down the corridor. She swept her left hand forward to give him the go-ahead. He picked up his briefcase and followed her. When Thag walked past the receptionist, she didn't look up from the passage she was reading from her pocket New Testament.

At the end of the hall he came to the corner office where the door stood open.

"It's an open door, not an open mind," Jewel said. "He's not his father's child."

Thag entered and saw Rudd Brightwell, Jr. standing next to the window. He looked like a trader on the floor of the New York Stock Exchange on a day the market was crashing. He wore his brown hair in a John Edwards cut. His manicured nails were a perfect fit for the soft white skin of his hands, hands that had never seen a hard day's labor. At five-feet eight-inches, he had a compact build with muscles toned by three times a week sessions with a personal trainer named Sugar Beets. He was clean-shaven but already had a five o'clock shadow at eleven fifteen in the morning.

His coat and tie hung on a hall tree behind his desk. He had the long sleeves of his white cotton shirt rolled mid way up his forearms to show off the muscle definition.

An unlighted cigarette dangled between the middle and index fingers of his left hand, and Brightwell played with his father's 1940s vintage Zippo lighter in his right while he talked. He held the phone against his shoulder with his neck muscles. A long white phone cord stretched almost beyond its tensile strength tethered him to his desk, its curly circles flattened out by Rudd's nervous energy that pulled him against it as he strained to see everything that happened on the city street below him.

Rudd pointed at a chair while he talked and Thag slumped down in the seat and waited for him to finish his conversation.

"Damn straight. Don't you forget it either," he said as he slammed the phone down, jumped in his chair and lit his cigarette. He picked the pack up off his desk and offered one to Thag.

"Don't mind if I do," Thag said.

They sat and smoked for a minute without talking.

"Woody Wilson?" Rudd said after a while.

"You need to cut him loose, Rudd. This is the sort of man you praise every year when you speak at Honor America Night out at the football stadium. My God, he fought in the Battle of the Bulge. On top of that, he has Alzheimer's. He had been abducted and thought he was on his way to rescue his wife. Do you really think a jury would convict him?" Thag didn't hold anything back.

"They will convict him if I tell them to," Rudd said. "I won't stand for anyone pulling a gun on one of my officers."

"He thought your officer was one of the bad guys, Rudd."

"He knew Deputy Hansen well enough to know he was no threat to him. His actions were unjustified," Rudd said.

"He's not even competent to stand trial," Thag said.

"I'll bet my psychiatrist will find that he knows right from wrong. That's all I need in order to put him to trial."

"Why would you do that, Rudd? His wife is prepared to care for him under house arrest for the rest of his life. Isn't that enough? He'll never threaten anyone again."

"He sure won't. Because he will be in the penitentiary, locked away from law-abiding citizens," Rudd said.

"You've got to be kidding me. You want to send Woody Wilson to the pen for life? What's gotten into you? I thought your dad taught you better than that."

At the mention of his father, Rudd got up and walked to a picture that hung on the wall nearest the door. A gray-haired man in a seersucker suit stood on the courthouse steps next to several judges in their black robes.

"Just because he held this office before me, doesn't mean I am like him. He got too soft in his old age. He didn't understand that people need swift, sure punishment."

"I tried a lot of cases against him, Rudd. Your dad knew when to let someone up off the mat and when to let the hammer down. He wasn't afraid to do either."

"Maybe that's the difference between me and him, Thag. I'm here to let the hammer down. You'll have to look for mercy somewhere else."

Thag rose from his chair, picked up his briefcase. He stood eye to eye with Rudd.

"I prefer to call it justice," he said. "I'll have my pre-trial motions filed by tomorrow afternoon."

"Go to church if you want forgiveness, Thag. I'll see you in court."

Thag walked out of the DA's office, his shoulders slumped. He concentrated on the carpet just in front of where he would step next. Jewel saw the look on his face and looked down at random sheets of paper on her desk until he passed her by and walked out the waiting room door. He rode the elevator to the third floor where the door opened and three lawmen stepped in. Thag caught a quick glimpse of Deputy Hansen's name tag. When they reached the ground floor, he trailed behind Hansen until he parted ways with the other officers.

"Deputy Hansen, I'm Thag Clemons. I represent Woody Wilson."

The deputy took his cap off for a minute, brushed his hair back with the palm of his left hand and re-placed the cap.

"How's Mr. Woody doing?" he said.

"He's a scared old man, son," Thag said.

"I really can't talk about the case with you, Mr. Clemons. Rudd Brightwell would have my ass if he saw us." Hansen looked around the parking lot and glanced at the building to be sure he wasn't where Brightwell could see him from his office window.

"I understand, son. I just wanted you to know that I will do what I can to look out for Mr. Wilson's interests," Clemons said.

Deputy Hansen nodded at Thag, then turned and walked toward the farthest point in the parking lot. He never looked back.

Thag limped to his car as if his briefcase threw him off balance. He tossed his valise through the front passenger window and leaned against the hood while he smoked a Camel. About sixty yards ahead of him and to his left he could see the rec yard of the county jail. There amid the off-scouring of the earth stood a thin old man. His fingers poked through the chain link fence of the enclosure as he held himself upright. He kicked the pavement with the toe of his right shoe.

As Thag watched, a dust devil blew through the rec yard. It swirled its dusty cone and made a direct hit on Woody, who opened his arms and allowed it to turn him around and around, as he danced like a child caught in a summer squall with his church clothes on. Finally the cyclone released him as it made its way through the chain link fence, where it dissipated in the free world before it reached Thag.

Clemons turned his back so the inmate couldn't make out his face. He put himself in the Corolla, started the engine and idled out of the parking lot, across the street and around the corner. He pulled into the deserted parking lot of a Presbyterian church, left his foot on the brake and reached under the driver's seat for the bottle he knew was there. He followed the first slug with a second and a third. Then he threw the empty whiskey bottle out the window and listened as it shattered against the pavement.

He abandoned his car for the night, staggered to the curb and hailed the first cab that came along.

"I suppose you want to go home, Mr. Clemons?" the cabby said as he looked over his right shoulder at his regular customer.

But Thag Clemons didn't answer him because he was already asleep in the back seat, where he dreamed of the coldest German winter on record and boys who killed each other not knowing why, while they yearned for their sweethearts back home and prayed for wool socks.

Chapter 24

WHEN FBI AGENTS arrived at the house in Fort Walton, they strung yellow evidence tape on metal stakes along 180 feet of the street on the front side of the property and posted dour guards to scour at passersby. By the time the feds went to work on the gravesites, Shot Glass Reynolds had already formulated his opinions.

Reynolds walked over to the senior CSI for the FBI, a thirty-five-ish hotshot named Omar Cuspid.

"You want to know what I think, Omar?" he asked.

"What if I said no?"

"Wouldn't matter," Reynolds said.

"I thought not."

"The body in the older of the two graves is the guy who lived here for years. I'm pretty sure he was Linus Schmutzer's uncle. Probably aren't any obits or other notices of his death. But I bet his will says he wants to be buried here."

"You're pretty sure? You got any proof?" Cuspid said.

"I'm relying on my finely honed investigative skills. They seldom fail me."

The CSI rolled his eyes and looked at the agents as they excavated the site. He started to walk away from Reynolds, but Reynolds kept talking.

"I'll bet you a hundred bucks the other guy is a shrink named Richard Davis. He used to work at the Middle Tennessee Mental Health Institute, left a few months ago to take a sabbatical in Pensacola, never showed up there."

Shot Glass stuck out his hand so Omar could shake on the wager. Cuspid looked at the agents as they dug their holes, glanced at Reynolds. He didn't bite on the bet.

"I think you may be a little ahead of me on this one, Detective Reynolds. But even if you're right about the IDs, what motive would Schmutzer have to murder the shrink? From what I saw in the file, Schmutzer is, or used to be anyway, a shrink himself."

"I'm still working on that part of the equation, but I think it has something to do with a World War Two vet with Alzheimer's named Woody Wilson. Schmutzer somehow lured him to Nashville and kidnapped him."

"I suppose you're *pretty sure* of that, too?"

"Yeah."

"Where's Wilson now?" Omar asked.

"In the Walton County jail charged with attempted capital murder of a police officer."

The CSI scratched his head.

"Don't tell me anything else. I need to keep an open mind while I'm working," he said.

"Work on this. Woody Wilson is innocent. He wasn't doing anything but protecting his wife from an imminent threat,"

Reynolds said before the crime scene investigator could turn away from him. "If you do your job right, we'll be able to prove it."

"*Imminent* is a big word for a jake legged temporary special investigator from Nashville. I don't need you to tell me how to do my job, Reynolds. Get out of my face," the FBI man said.

"I guess they don't have a course in bedside manners at the FBI Academy," Reynolds snapped back at him.

The CSI turned his back on Reynolds and walked to the gravesites. The agents who dug the holes had stopped shoveling dirt when they reached body bags at a depth of four feet.

Ground water seeped in the earthen pits, and the men bailed it out like sailors trying to keep a sinking ship afloat. Agents sloshed in the mud at either end of the bodies, stuck their arms under the cadavers' heads and feet and hoisted them out on dry ground next to the holes.

The investigator who had dissed Reynolds strapped a white gauze mask on his face with elastic bands wrapped around his ears, donned a pair of surgical gloves and unzipped the bag from the older grave. Inside he found a decomposed body of an old man. Next to it in the death cocoon was a plastic Ziploc baggie that protected some papers. He opened the baggie and pulled out a document.

"It's a death certificate of one Linus Schmutzer," he said. He drew out another sheaf of about ten pages of paper. He looked at the first page. "The Last Will and Testament of Linus Schmutzer," he read.

He shot a glance at Reynolds who stood behind him.

"Imagine that," Shot Glass said.

The CSI put the papers back in the baggie, zipped it closed. He walked to the other body bag and unzipped it. Inside he found the body of a male in his late fifties a few months dead. A sports jacket draped the cadaver. Khaki pants lay against the rotted lower part of the corpse. The shoes still held an unblemished shine.

The jacket bulged against the skeleton as it lay on the rib cage. The CSI opened the jacket, put his hand in the inside coat pocket and pulled out a leather wallet. It contained five credit cards, a Tennessee driver license and three business cards. He looked at one of the business cards, hesitated for a second, then handed it over his shoulder to Reynolds who had watched his every move.

Shot Glass read the business card, "Richard Davis, M.D., Psychiatrist."

"If he wanted to hide this body, he didn't do a very good job. He buried him in a shallow grave, left his ID on him and put the property up for sale. He had to know someone would stumble on the graves before long," the CSI said.

Reynolds walked back and forth between the bodies. He looked down at the ground and then gazed out into the bay. He breathed in the salt air. In a minute he came back into the moment.

"He's taunting us. I've seen a few like him through the years. They're usually some really bad sumbitches."

"I figured as much," the CSI said. "You have any idea where to find him?"

Reynolds appreciated the question. It meant the CSI thought Shot Glass knew what he was doing. "Not a clue, yet. But I'm pretty sure he knows we're here and knows we won't be too far behind him. He's got something big up his sleeve."

The CSI walked over to Reynolds and shook his hand. "I didn't know what I was dealing with, Detective Reynolds. I hope I can help you nail this bastard."

"Hey, I'm an asshole. Everybody in Tennessee knows that. You just didn't get the memo. Keep up the good work, son. We'll get this guy."

Shot Glass turned and walked towards the sun room on the back of the house where Waylon Wilson had set up a mobile command post on a card table. He worked at his laptop while Reynolds badgered the FBI.

"Did you find out anything you didn't know already?" Waylon asked him when he got close to the porch.

"It's pretty much what we suspected. The bodies belong to Linus Schmutzer, the old man, and Dr. Richard Davis, who never made it to his sabbatical. Linus the younger appears to be a fairly ruthless character."

Waylon listened to the report. He looked back at his computer screen and closed out a couple of Internet investigations he had started.

"So what sort of stuff had Linus the Second been into before he kidnapped my dad?"

Reynolds could see that Waylon was near his breaking point.

"I don't know yet, Waylon. He's an enigma. At least your dad is out from under his influence."

"I wouldn't go that far. Guys like Schmutzer somehow exert an influence much greater than they deserve."

Just then Waylon's Blackberry buzzed in his belt holster. He reached down and took it out, scanned the new messages. He looked at the first item on the list, double-clicked on the link, waited for the page to load.

"You're not going to believe this," he said to Reynolds.

"Try me."

"I just received a Google alert on Linus Schmutzer."

"A what?"

"A Google alert. You go to Google, put in a word or phrase you want to monitor and every time something appears on the Internet that contains the key word or phrase it pops up on your e-mail. I put 'Linus Schmutzer' in as an alert three weeks ago. This is my first hit."

"What's it say?" Shot Glass said.

"It's a first-hand account of the life and death of Linus Schmutzer," Waylon said.

Waylon went to his laptop and entered the link. On the screen appeared a clear image of the property at Ft. Walton and two men engaged in conversation.

"That's a picture of us about three minutes ago," Reynolds said. "Who claims to be the author?"

"Linus Schmutzer the Second," Waylon said as he stood up and looked behind him in the direction where the camera must have been to get the shot. He saw nothing but cop cars.

Shot Glass ran to the street and looked both directions. He checked the trees to see if he could detect a hidden camera. When he found none he walked back to Waylon.

"He's slick," Reynolds said.

"Wait 'til you read the article," Waylon said. He turned his laptop so Reynolds could see the screen and waited while Shot Glass read the fresh diary entry of Linus Schmutzer II, a sociopath turned psychiatrist, who had graduated to murder.

Chapter 25

WHEN THAG CLEMONS filed his motion to determine if Woody Wilson was competent to stand trial, Rudd Brightwell, Jr., wasted no time scouting out the best qualified psychiatrist in the state of Florida who would always testify for the prosecution if need be. After a couple of phone calls to some fellow prosecutors, he got a good lead on the most talented whore psychiatrist in the state.

He dialed the number as he looked out his office window at the traffic jam on the street below him.

"Zebidiah Banks," the voice said on the other end of the line. It sounded muffled, almost like an electronically simulated human voice.

"Dr. Banks, this is Rudd Brightwell. I'm the DA in Walton County. I have a job for you, if you want it."

"I'm always ready to be of service to the people of Florida," Banks said.

"Good. You're in Tampa, aren't you?"

"That's right."

"I need you to pack your bags and come to the Panhandle for a couple of days. I'll make it worth your while."

"May I ask what my assignment is?" Banks said.

"I have an old guy here who held a gun on one of my deputies and now claims to have Alzheimer's. He knew exactly what he was doing, and because of it, he should stand trial in front of a jury, take his chances and go to the pen. Do you understand me, Dr. Banks?"

"You're coming through loud and clear, Mr. Brightwell."

"Okay. I'll find you an empty office here at the courthouse as an examination room, and we'll have the prisoner brought down to see you Monday morning. Give me a call when you arrive in Walton County, and we'll hook up." Brightwell gave him the number to his cell.

"I'll see you the first of the week, Mr. Brightwell," Banks said as he ended the call.

Rudd Brightwell, Jr., expected a call from Zebidiah Banks over the weekend, but he didn't hear from him until fifteen minutes after eight Monday morning. That was when he walked in the door at the DA's office and asked to see Rudd.

The receptionist had just finished hanging a new picture of her daughter on the wall behind her, a picture of her future son-in-law proposing marriage to her baby girl on the side of a mountain in the Ozarks. Behind the couple, who bowed their heads in prayer, a thirty-foot high wooden cross leaned against the face of the cliff. Painted in red on the limestone next to the cross were the words, "Get Right With God."

She looked Banks up and down.

He had a ponytail died black tied with a rubber band that hung low down his back. He never removed his aviator sunglasses, and his stark white facial skin looked like it had been stretched taut against his facial bones, like that of a man without a helmet riding a motorcycle 130 miles per hour. His pitch black eyebrows appeared to have been drawn on with a makeup pencil.

"The DA wanted to see me," Dr. Banks said. "I'm a psychiatrist from Tampa. My name is Zebidiah Banks."

"Not many folks talk to him while they're wearing sunglasses, Dr. Brinks," she said.

"It's Banks," the psychiatrist said.

"Just take a seat over there until I call you," she said.

Banks took a seat where she pointed. Then, he picked up his briefcase, pulled out a magazine and started reading.

"Jewel," the receptionist said. "There's a shrink here to see RBJ. He says he's come up from Tampa. His name is Banks."

"Let me check it out with Rudd," Jewel said.

Dr. Banks noticed that while he waited, the receptionist stared at the skin of his face, intrigued that it looked like bleached latex. He was used to such furtive glances.

In a minute or so, Jewel called back.

"Tell him to come on down," she said.

The receptionist hung up the phone, straightened the papers on her desk, and took another look at the photograph. She stood up and re-positioned the photograph of the recently affianced couple. She sat down.

"Dr. Brinks, the DA will see you now," she said.

She didn't look at him when she spoke because she sensed in her spirit that he was both a pervert and a liberal.

"Thanks, Ms. Glasscock," Banks said as he passed the receptionist.

She had hidden her name plate behind a stack of file folders.

"It's Mrs. Glasscock, Dr. Brinks," the receptionist said.

"I was burned in a house fire years ago. Maybe the folks at your church will pray for me if you ask them," he said as he passed by her guard post.

The receptionist turned away from the psychiatrist.

Before he got out of ear shot, he heard her say under her breath, "I doubt it, Zeb."

Rudd Brightwell, Jr., shook hands with Dr. Banks and invited him to take a seat in one of the large armed chairs that sat in front of his father's antique oak desk. The DA sized him up for a minute before he spoke.

"You don't wear those sunglasses when you testify, do you, Doc?" he asked.

"The last three years I wear them all the time," Dr. Banks said. "My eyes went bad as a result of my diabetes. The jury loves to hear from a sick doctor. It brings me down to the level of common folks."

"I never thought of it that way," Rudd said.

"Believe me, it works."

"I hope so, Dr. Banks. Woody Wilson needs those jurors to pop his ass for about a ninety-nine-year sentence. Do you think you can provide me that kind of psychiatric fire power?"

"Unless Mr. Wilson sprouts wings and flies out of prison, you shouldn't have to worry about him anymore, Mr. Brightwell. Wilson is faking it, and I will show you and the jury how I know."

"Okay, Doc. I will need a full report from you no later than Wednesday afternoon."

"You'll have my report by the end of business Wednesday," Banks said.

He got up from the chair, walked out Rudd's office door and passed along the hallway until he reached the receptionist's desk.

"Tell your daughter the Lord wants her to take good care of that young man every day for the rest of their lives come rain or shine, in good times or bad. She must be to him what the scriptures call a helpmeet," he said as he admired the new picture.

Mrs. Glasscock looked puzzled as if she had misread the psychiatrist. "I will tell her, Dr. Banks. It's nice to meet a doctor who understands the things of God," she said as she fiddled with the picture one more time to make sure it hung straight.

"And tell her she needs to screw him every night just for extra measure," Banks said as he walked out the lobby door. His high-pitched, mechanical laugh echoed off the marble floor as he made his way to the elevator.

The receptionist put her hands over her ears and closed her eyes. She took the picture down from the wall and placed it on her lap while she prayed that God would protect her and her daughter from vile men like Dr. Zebidiah Banks.

Chapter 26

AT TEN O'CLOCK sharp, Deputy Bart walked Woody down a long hallway and stopped in front of an old wooden door with a pane of opaque glass, wrinkled like elephant skin. He took Woody inside the makeshift examining room where Dr. Banks sat behind a fungible government desk. He removed Woody's handcuffs and withdrew to the hallway to stand guard during the interview.

"Have a seat, Mr. Wilson," Dr. Banks said when Woody entered the room.

"My name is Woodrow Wilson. But folks 'round here call me Mr. Woody," Woody said as he stuck out his hand to the psychiatrist.

Banks ignored Woody's hand and motioned for him to take a seat in the chair in front of his desk. "The DA hired me to evaluate your competence to stand trial, Mr. Wilson," Banks said. "Anything you tell me in this room is admissible as evidence against you. Do you understand why you're here?"

"You may have to explain it a little more to me, Doc," Woody said. He looked uneasy with the setting, glanced around the room like a man trapped in a chamber while water began to flood it.

"Do you know why you're in jail?"

"I had a run in with Deputy Hansen. He's a good boy. I didn't mean him no harm," Woody said.

"Have you met with your lawyer? A man named Pythagoras Clemons?" Banks said.

Woody thought for a minute. "Pythagoras? Oh, you mean Thag. Yeah. I met with him. I like that name Thag for a lawyer. He and I are going to make a good team, the A-team, Thag said."

Banks opened a folder in front of him on the desk, took a fountain pen from his shirt pocket, screwed the top off it. He tested it on a blank piece of paper to be sure it had ink in it.

"Okay, Mr. Wilson. If you will answer a couple of more questions for me we'll have you out of here in a jiffy," Banks said.

"Fire away," Woody said.

"Who is the President of the United States?" Banks asked.

Woody stared at the doctor a few seconds before he replied. "Didn't vote for him; don't give a damn," he said.

Banks made a note on the pad in the folder.

"How many kids do you have, Mr. Wilson?"

Woody could feel anger begin to boil in his stomach. It worked its way up his throat. He tried to strangle it before it flowed out his mouth. "Didn't they tell you anything about me before you came in here?"

The psychiatrist wrote something else down without ever making eye contact with Woody. He laid the pen down.

"This will go a lot quicker if you just try to answer my questions, Mr. Wilson. Arguing with me won't get us anywhere."

"I wasn't arguing. I thought you already knew the answer, that's all." Woody looked around to see if Deputy Bart was still in the room.

"The jailer is waiting outside. I'll call him when it's time for you to go."

"Bart's wife just had her baby," Woody said.

"I see," Banks said.

Woody got up out of the chair and began to pace. He went to the door and grabbed the handle, tried to twist it.

"It's locked, Mr. Wilson. You're stuck with me for the time being."

Woody stared at the door handle for a minute, then walked to the chair and sat down again.

"If you must know, I have one boy, Waylon. He's a computer genius. Not much of a fisherman though," Woody said. He began to laugh like he was sharing a joke with the doctor, but he caught himself.

Banks didn't smile.

"Where do you live, Mr. Wilson?" Banks asked.

Woody looked at the doctor wide-eyed like an old steer trapped in a de-horning pen.

"I live at the condo with Maggie, but I'm visiting my friends here for a little while."

"Which friends?"

"Odd Sheffield and Theo. We plan to do some fishing one of these days soon," Woody said.

Banks took a few more notes.

"Are you married?" Banks asked.

Woody's face flattened.

He ducked his head, then exploded.

"What have you done with Maggie?" Woody said as he stood up and pushed his body against the desk. He reached out both arms to grab Dr. Banks, but Banks rolled his chair away from the desk so that Woody missed him and had to catch himself when he fell forward onto the top of the desk.

"Sit down, Mr. Wilson," Banks said. His voice was stern, his tone uncompromising. He acted like this sort of encounter was nothing new to him.

Woody raised himself off the desk with both hands. When he regained his footing, his hands trembled. He teetered and collapsed in the chair.

"What have you done with Maggie?" Woody repeated. He was crying now.

On the wall behind Banks hung an old clock, its face a dingy yellow, its numbers black and worn out from years of relentless service. The second hand, which knew not how to hurry, made a full revolution before either man said another word.

Dr. Banks twisted the top on his pen and placed it in his pocket, the only trace of the writing instrument, a chrome clip, cold against the white cotton. Then he put several loose sheets of paper into a folder and flipped it closed. He bent over and stuck the file in his briefcase.

"Maggie is fine, Mr. Wilson. I'm sure she will come to visit you later today."

Woody loosened his grip on the arms of the chair. He closed his eyes and let his chin drop near his chest as he took a deep breath and exhaled like a condemned man on the day of his execution.

"Those are all the questions I have for you today, Mr.

Wilson. That wasn't too bad, was it?" Banks said.

"I guess not, Doc Smooth," Woody said as he got up to leave.

"My name is Dr. Banks," the psychiatrist said. He didn't get up or look at Woody as the old man made his way to the door. "I'll see you in court, Mr. Wilson."

Deputy Bart opened the door when he heard Woody knock. He escorted him out into the hallway and closed the door behind him without a word to the psychiatrist.

Dr. Banks waited a couple of minutes before he walked to the door, opened it and checked the corridor to make sure Woody was gone.

Then he went back to his loaner desk, leaned back in his chair, picked up a handheld digital recorder and began to dictate his report.

"Although Woody Wilson exhibits some of the classic symptoms of stage 3 Alzheimer's, his overall demeanor contradicts such a diagnosis. My opinion, in reasonable medical probability, is that he is a malingerer and charlatan who uses the guise of Alzheimer's when it suits his purposes. He understands the nature of the charges against him and has a clear grasp of the difference between right and wrong. He is competent to stand trial and assist his attorney in his defense."

He switched the recorder off and dropped it in his valise.

"Don't worry, Woody. I'll take good care of you," he said as he stood up and walked out of the room. He left the door to his makeshift office open on his way out and didn't bother to stop by to see Rudd Brightwell before he began his drive back to Tampa.

Chapter 27

AT FIRST LIGHT Maggie got in her ten year old Land Cruiser with 225,000 miles on it and drove four miles north towards Choctawhatchee Bay on Highway 395. She rolled the windows down and smelled the ocean as it gave way to the bay. She passed the entrance to Eden State Park on her left, its grounds blocked by a stand of virgin timber draped in the tentacles of Spanish moss.

When she got to Point Washington, she turned right into the parking lot of an old Methodist church just a few hundred yards before the road dipped into the backwaters of the bay at the public boat ramp. She thought about that landing where Woody had so often brought the *Miss Maggie* around to pick her up.

"All aboard that's coming aboard," he used to say to her as he swung the Parker boat next to the pier. Before she got out of her car, she studied the church of her childhood, a simple white frame sanctuary which in its imposing innocence marked a stark line of demarcation between the things of this world and the next.

She walked around the back of the church and lifted the latch on the chain link gate to the cemetery where the faithful and faithless lay side by side in an eternal truce.

Careful not to disturb the spirits, she walked in the middle of the grass footpaths that criss-crossed the cemetery until she came to a familiar spot that lay in the shade of an oak tree eight feet around at the trunk.

The marble border with the name Gilbert etched in it was the only thing that segregated her progenitors from all the others who had gone on ahead of her.

She pulled on a pair of gardening gloves, got down on her hands and knees and picked weeds from the base of the headstones, wiped dead leaves off the granite monuments of her father and mother.

She gazed at an empty section on the south side of the plot, an area large enough for only two more graves.

"It will be just the right place for you and me, Woody," she said. Then with her shoe, she traced a rectangle in the dirt where she thought the caskets could fit. When she finished, she looked at the spot one last time, stuck her gloves in her coat pocket and marched out of the necropolis.

When she got to Highway 98, she turned east toward Panama City. A mile down the road, she found Walton Monuments and drove to the parking place nearest the small metal shack she took to be the office.

When she entered the office, she saw a gray-haired man about her age, wearing a dark green wool jacket with frayed cuffs, seated at a beat up wooden desk cluttered with stacks of paper. He had his brown horn-rimmed bifocals perched on his forehead while he wrote figures on a note pad with a lead pencil. He didn't look up until he completed his task.

"Yes, ma'am," he said. He stared at her, cocked his head, adjusted his glasses on his nose to get a better look at her.

"Can I look at some headstones?" Maggie said.

The old man got up from his desk, walked around and positioned himself less than a foot in front of Maggie.

She didn't give way.

"It's been a long time since the high school dance hasn't it, Maggie Gilbert?" he said. His gray eyebrows moved closer together, his milky brown eyes tried to sparkle.

Maggie looked up at him and thought back to a church fellowship hall decked with banners that announced the graduating class of Eden High School, 1943. A hardwood floor separated a line of girls against one wall, anxious young men against the other. From the middle of the boys' line, a dark-haired, skinny boy, already wearing the brown dress uniform of a United States Army buck private, broke ranks and approached her. She looked at the floor and hoped he would change course mid-stream, but he never faltered.

"I would be honored if you would dance with me, Miss Gilbert," he said. He reached out his hand to take hers. With no place to hide, she glanced at the girl next to her who was checking out the ceiling fans. Trapped, she placed her hand in the boy's sweaty palm.

"The pleasure would be all mine, Mr. Cumberland," she said. And they danced, four minutes, maybe five, that one time, more than sixty years before.

"Hank Cumberland," she said and gave him a hug. He was not so skinny anymore.

"They were playing *That Old Black Magic.* I've been under your spell ever since. You were the prettiest girl I ever saw, and now you're the most beautiful full grown woman on the face of God's green earth." Hank squeezed her tight against him with his left arm and pivoted her around him like they were still dancing to that old song. He leaned over and pecked her on the forehead, then released her. He was embarrassed, but proud he had seized the moment, one that he knew would never come again.

"You'll have to forgive an old fool," he said.

"The pleasure was all mine, Mr. Cumberland," Maggie said. And they stood together in the tombstone office and thought about what might have been until Maggie broke the silence.

"Hank, I am going to need a double headstone, probably in the near future," she said.

He took her left hand with his right and led her out the door to a golf cart beside the metal hut. "If you'll get in my chariot, I'll give you the tour," he said. Hank drove down two rows of headstones until he came to a collection of monuments near the far corner of the lot.

"These are the double ones. They are not as popular as they used to be." His quiet resolve muted the humor in his words.

Maggie got out of the golf cart and walked along the carved chunks of granite. As she browsed, she placed her hand on the top of each stone and felt its ineluctable, unforgiving, certainty.

She pointed at a plain rose-hued headstone. "I'll need to give you the inscription, Hank. Woody won't be up to it when the time comes."

"I'll chisel them myself by hand, Maggie. I'll make it look real nice for you and Mr. Wilson. I'm sorry I never got to meet him. He must be a helluva man."

"He is, Hank. He is."

Maggie got back in the golf cart, and Hank drove them to the office. He tore a sheet of paper off a yellow legal pad and handed it and his pencil to her. She put the paper on the desk top and while she stood wrote a couple of lines, folded the paper in two and handed it back to him.

"I'll take care of it when the time comes," Hank said.

"I'm so glad it was you," she said.

"The pleasure was all mine, Mrs. Wilson," Hank said.

Maggie got in her car and idled through the headstones until she came to the back corner of the lot again. She rolled her window down and looked at the stone one more time. Then she pulled out on the highway and turned west.

It was almost visiting time at Walton County jail.

Chapter 28

WHEN SHOT GLASS finished reading the article by Linus Schmutzer II, he stood with his right hand on his chin, his eyes focused on the ground.

"Print it out for me," he said to Waylon.

"I don't have a printer here; I'll have to go to Kwik Copy," Waylon said.

"Print it out," Reynolds said again. "I can't read between the lines on a computer monitor."

Waylon copied the file to his flash drive, extracted the drive from the USB port, dropped it in his pocket and headed towards his car in the driveway.

By the time Waylon got back from the print shop, Reynolds had outlined Schmutzer's family tree with a Sharpie on brown butcher paper spread out on a picnic table in the back yard. The FBI agents were still digging in the mud near the graves. They paid no attention to Reynolds.

Waylon tossed two copies of the article on the table.

Reynolds moved them to the side while he finished his diagram. He stepped back from the table and looked at his work.

"That's about the size of it, I reckon," he said. Then he picked up a broken branch from the grass and wielded it in his left hand like a teacher making his point on the blackboard. He began the lesson.

"Reinhold Schmutzer was the patriarch. He made his fortune distilling corn whiskey in Tennessee. When he had twin sons, he wanted them to enjoy the benefits of wealth, so he shipped them back to the fatherland to receive their formal education."

"I thought you couldn't process stuff from a computer screen," Waylon said.

"I lied. I needed a few minutes alone to work through the details."

Waylon glanced down at the paper on the table.

"Continue," he said.

"The twin boys were Horatio and Linus, born March 5, 1919. That would have made them 14 years old when Hitler became Prime Minister in '33. It was a helluva time to start their higher education in Germany. According to Linus, he and his brother took to their lessons like pigs to mud. The next thing you know they are sitting for their entrance exams for medical school."

"It was also about the time an Austrian doctor named Sigmund Freud began to chart the dark recesses of the human mind," Waylon said.

Reynolds nodded.

"Psychoanalysis," Shot Glass said. "My ex-wife told me I needed some of that."

Waylon picked up a copy of the article and thumbed through it. "Apparently the brothers Schmutzer got caught up in it, too. They both became psychiatrists. But by the time the war broke out, they had reached a dividing point," he said.

Reynolds touched the branch to the paper.

"Horatio opposed the Nazis; Linus joined them," he said.

"It's almost like the American Civil War, brother against brother," Waylon said.

"Except that the Schmutzer brothers came together not on the battlefield, but in the prison house of the soul, a camp called Auschwitz."

"Linus was the camp physician, Horatio an inmate. Can you imagine it?" Waylon said.

"No. I can't," Reynolds said.

"Daddy was one of the first GIs in there," Waylon said. "He never talked about the details much, but he said he made friends with one of the survivors. I think they corresponded until his friend passed away."

Reynolds thought about the time line.

"When did his friend die?" he asked.

"Before I was born."

"When was that?"

"April 23, 1960."

Shot Glass went to his briefcase and took out his case file on Woody Wilson. He found a folder with a few pictures in it, pulled out the one of Maggie and Woody with the man they visited at the country house near Franklin.

"The article says Linus returned to America after the war. But you have already searched every record known to man for some mention of him and come up empty. If he was a concentration camp doctor, he should have been tried for war crimes," Reynolds said. "If he came back, he must have assumed another identity."

"Like Joseph Mengele," Waylon said.

"Something like that," Reynolds said. "The sorry sumbitch."

"You don't think he was daddy's friend, do you?" Waylon said as he glanced at the black and white print.

"No. You said Woody's friend was an Auschwitz survivor. That has to be Horatio." Reynolds tapped his right index finger on the face of the third person in the picture. "Your dad and mom visited him in the fall of '57. Linus the younger was born in May of '58."

"And his mother died in childbirth," Waylon added.

Reynolds cocked his head and looked at a grackle that was squawking in an oak tree.

"Horatio has a son and a dead wife in May, 1958. By April, 1960, he is dead, too, and we have no record of what happened to him."

"You're the trained investigator, but it strikes me that one common characteristic of twin brothers is that they look alike," Waylon said.

"Yeah, I lived across the street from a couple of identical twins when I was a kid. Whenever either one of them pissed me off, I gave both of them an ass-whipping to be sure I had the bases covered," Shot Glass said.

Waylon laughed and looked over at the FBI agents who thought it was something at their expense.

Reynolds closed his file and put it back in his briefcase, snapped the latch shut.

He turned to Waylon. "Okay, Detective Wilson. I suppose you have deduced the following. Linus Schmutzer, a Nazi war criminal in hiding, seizes on his brother's death, sneaks into the country and assumes his identity. As some sort of family trade off to protect his scheme, he agrees to raise Horatio's orphaned son, Linus the Second. Linus the Second follows in his uncle's footsteps, becomes a psychiatrist and uses his patients as guinea pigs."

"Something like that," Waylon said. "But that still doesn't explain Linus the younger's connection to my dad."

Reynolds picked up his briefcase and began walking toward his car. Waylon trailed behind him waiting for him to speak. When they got to Reynolds' car, Shot Glass threw his case in the back seat and leaned against the driver's door.

"I think it does. Get in. We're going to the jail to see your dad. I need to talk to him about something."

"What?"

"Atonement," Shot Glass said as he jerked the car away from the house and knocked down the FBI's yellow tape.

Chapter 29

ON THE WAY to the jail, Shot Glass took out his cell phone and called Thag Clemons at home. The phone rang six times, seven, eight without an answer. Reynolds let it ring. On about the fifteenth ring, Thag came on the line.

"Who the hell is it?" he said.

"Thag. It's Shot Glass Reynolds."

"Yeah?"

"Woody Wilson's son and I are on our way to the jail to see him. I thought I ought to let you know since you are his lawyer and all," Reynolds said.

"Where are you now?"

"We're just crossing the bridge at the east pass."

"Good. That'll give me enough time. I need to see him, too. I'll meet you in the visitors lobby at the jail."

The line went dead.

Twenty minutes later, Shot Glass and Waylon were seated in the waiting area when Clemons walked in. He had on a plaid flannel shirt with chicken grease stains on the front, a pair of polyester slacks, and New Balance running shoes with no shoe strings. He had a three-day growth of beard and a four-day no shower smell.

Thag dropped his briefcase on the floor with a thud, stuck out his hand to shake with Waylon and looked sideways at Shot Glass.

"I need to talk to him about the motion for a psychiatric examination. I just received a copy of the shrink's report this morning," he said to both of them. "I don't care if we go in together if you think he can stand all three of us at once."

Waylon and Shot Glass nodded.

Thag went to the window where a female deputy sheriff tended the entrance to the cell block. Her hair, dyed yellow and cropped to one inch, was pasted tight to her scalp by some kind of wax.

She had a half-empty Whataburger chocolate shake next to the phone. Her rear end lopped over both sides of her rolling desk chair.

"What can I do for you, Mr. Clemons?" she asked.

"Charlize, these men here are friends of mine and Mr. Woody." He pronounced the *ch* in Charlize like the first two letters in *charbroiled*. He pointed at Shot Glass and Waylon. Reynolds winked, smiled and gave her a small salute. "We have some business to discuss with him," Thag said.

"You know we aren't supposed to let more than one visitor in at a time, Thag."

"Except for exceptional circumstances, Char. The sheriff let me bring five people in to see Gorilla Hopkins one time."

"That's 'cause Gorilla told everybody he was going to whip your ass the next time he saw you," she said.

Thag laughed. "He might have done it, too, if I hadn't planned ahead."

"These folks are Woody's son and a detective from Nashville. The sheriff wouldn't object to either of them," Thag said.

Charlize looked at Shot Glass and Waylon.

"I reckon not," Charlize said. "I'll ring Deputy Bart and tell him to put y'all in the conference room." She punched a button and the latch on the steel door clicked open.

"Thanks, Hon. I'll see you at Sally's Back Side Thursday night," Thag said.

"I'll save you a seat," she said as he walked through the door. "And bring that Tennessee detective with you."

The three men walked down the hall toward the holding cell.

"Have you always been that irresistible to the fairer sex, Reynolds?" Thag asked.

"I'm particularly desired by the undesirable," Shot Glass said as he looked straight ahead.

Deputy Bart met them at the end of the hall. "Char said something about the conference room?"

"Yeah, we need some room to spread out," Thag said.

Deputy Bart waved for them to follow behind him.

When he reached the last room at the end of the hallway, he held the brass ring on his belt close to the lock and inserted a master key.

"I'll have Mr. Woody down here in a few minutes," he said as they filed into the room. He locked the door behind him when he left.

Thag propped his feet on a metal chair with a plastic seat cushion and leaned his head back.

"Do you want to hear about the psych eval?" he asked as if he were speaking into the air above his head.

Waylon took the bait. "I'd like to know what they said about my dad." He had been quiet since Thag's encounter with Charlize in the waiting room.

Thag looked at him and considered how to break the news. "I don't mean to offend you, Waylon. I think your dad is one of the greatest men I have ever known."

"That's okay. I want to hear what the doctor said."

"Well, you need to understand that the doctor in this case is an expert hired by the DA to dump shit on your dad," Thag said. "He isn't a disinterested doc who looked at him without bias."

"I understand the game, Thag. Just tell us what he said," Waylon said.

"He said your dad was as competent to stand trial as Ronald Reagan was to be President of the United States of America," Thag said.

"What do you mean?" Waylon asked.

"The whole world knows now that Reagan had Alzheimer's disease. Did anyone ever mention it when he was the most powerful man in the free world?" Thag asked Waylon.

"No. We learned about it later," Waylon said.

"That's what I mean," Thag said. "The shrink knows your dad has Alzheimer's, but he isn't going to tell the world until it's too late. The system is designed to hide Alzheimer's from public view. It isn't an acceptable explanation for anything. We all believe it won't come calling at our houses, that we are immune to it."

"It's like my Uncle Pete. He came to visit us when I was eight years old. I didn't get my bed back until I was fifteen,"

Shot Glass said. Waylon wasn't buying it.

"Alzheimer's is the explanation for the whole situation," Waylon said. He couldn't grasp why the twenty-first century American legal system was stuck at a 1930s understanding of the disease.

He pushed both his hands down in the air as if he could somehow elevate himself above the situation. He pulled a chair out from against the wall and sat down next to Shot Glass.

Shot Glass patted Waylon on the back.

"Thag is trying to tell you that your dad is fucked," Reynolds said after a while.

"I understand," Waylon said. "But momma is never going to be able to accept it."

Before anyone could respond to Waylon's remarks, the three men heard the door to the conference room open. Woody stepped in.

His face, always thin, was now gaunt, covered in gray stubble. He held his arms close to his chest, his fists clenched, as if he were defending himself from punches in a fighting match against a larger and more powerful opponent. He looked around the room. His gaze passed quickly over Thag and Reynolds, but froze for a second on Waylon.

"Is this where they're having the meeting? Deputy Bart said there was a meeting going on," Woody said to all of them, to none of them.

"You're in the right place, Mr. Wilson," Waylon said.

Woody looked at him again. "Have we met, young man? You look familiar, but I can't quite place the face."

"It's been a while since we saw each other," Waylon lied. "I'm one of Maggie's friends."

"Any friend of Maggie's is a friend of mine. I'm Woodrow

Wilson, but most folks around here call me Mr. Woody." He stuck out his hand to Waylon.

"I'm Waylon," he said as he took Woody's hand.

Shot Glass and Thag wiped their eyes and looked away from the father and son.

"These are a couple of other friends of Maggie's. They have come here to visit with you a minute, Mr. Woody," Waylon said as he directed Woody's attention to Thag and Reynolds.

"It's a pleasure to meet you boys," Woody said as he shook hands with the other two men.

"Why don't you sit down for a minute, Mr. Wilson?" Thag said as he pointed to a chair next to the table.

When Woody took his seat, Clemons began. "I'm your lawyer, Thag Clemons."

"I never had a lawyer before. Do I need one?" Woody said.

"I'm afraid you do. You're in some trouble because of the deal at the Tom Thumb," Thag said.

He had been over this ground many times with Woody.

"What deal?" Woody asked.

"When you pulled the gun on the deputy," Thag explained his voice flat, his words deliberate.

Woody stared at Thag, scratched his head with his right hand. "I think you may have the wrong man, sir. I didn't do anything like that."

It was the first time since Thag had known Woody that the old man couldn't remember the incident with a little prodding from Thag. Thag knew when to break off the discussion.

"You may be right, Mr. Wilson. It might have been someone else," he said. He picked up the psychiatric report, folded it down the middle long ways and stuck it in his back pocket. Thag looked over at Reynolds and Waylon to signal them that he had finished his part of the conversation.

Shot Glass pulled a chair up next to Woody and sat down so that his face and Woody's were at the same level. He was less than a foot from Woody when he spoke to him like a father to his favorite son.

"Mr. Woody, do you remember a man you knew in the war named Horatio Schmutzer?" he asked.

The light returned to Woody's eyes for a second, then he began to cry. "He died too young. There's not a day that goes by when I don't think about him and miss him."

Woody was smiling now. "When he came out of the camp, he was skin and bones. I told him if he stood sideways and stuck out his tongue he'd look like a zipper."

Woody was crying again. "When he got back to Tennessee, his daddy tried to set him up a medical practice in Franklin. But Horatio couldn't get in step with the outside world again. I thought when he married June he might have turned the corner. When she died, it was the last straw. He loved his new son, but he just couldn't keep going."

Shot Glass and Waylon looked at each other, amazed that Woody could remember and articulate details from sixty years before, when he couldn't recognize his own son.

"What happened to him, Mr. Woody?" Waylon asked.

"The police said he killed himself, but I never believed it. It didn't make sense to me that a man who could survive Auschwitz would take his own life in the free world. I think that sorry brother of his had something to do with it," Woody said.

"You mean Linus?" Shot Glass asked.

When Reynolds said Linus' name, Woody jumped up

from his chair. He started to pace the room, his face red with anger.

"He was nothing but a cold-blooded killer. It's one thing to shoot a man in battle where it's you or him. It's another for a coward to torment helpless people. What sort of man could stand by and watch his brother waste away and never raise his hand to save him? I can't believe they let him raise Horatio's son."

"You knew about that?" Reynolds asked.

"I just heard about it. I never met Linus. If I had, I would have given him what he deserved," Woody said.

"What's that?" Waylon asked.

"A 45 bullet right between the eyes," Woody said. He felt for his pistol on his right hip, looked down at his side to see if he was armed. When he realized he didn't have his gun, he calmed down and took a seat in the chair.

"Horatio must have seen some good in his brother. He named his son after him." Shot Glass wanted to get to the bottom of it.

"That's just the way Horatio was. Even after all he went through, he never stopped believing in people. He wanted the young Linus to be as good as the old one was bad. That didn't work out either. Doc Smooth was a mixture of them both."

"You talk like you've known him for a while," Reynolds said.

"Ever since he was born is all. He would show up every now and then out of the blue. He said his daddy wanted him to keep tabs on me."

Thag was trying to follow the conversation. "Mr. Wilson, are you saying that you had known the man who kidnapped you for a long time?"

"Kidnapped me? When?" Woody said.

"A couple of weeks ago from a hotel parking lot in Nashville, Mr. Woody," Shot Glass said.

Woody wrinkled his forehead as he tried to remember.

"I think I need to get back to my room now," he said. "Maggie will be here in a little while."

He got up and went to the door, pounded on it three times. "That's my signal for Deputy Bart," he said.

In a minute, the men heard a key turn in the latch and Deputy Bart swung the door open. Woody waved at them as he walked out the door. "I enjoyed the meeting," he said as he turned and walked down the corridor.

"I'll be back in a minute to let y'all out," Bart said as he locked the conference room door again.

When the three men got outside, they walked to Thag's car. Thag opened the driver's side front door, sat down in the driver's seat, let his feet hang out on the pavement. Waylon and Shot Glass stood on either side of him while they talked.

"I thought I understood this case. I was wrong," Thag said.

"You and me both," Shot Glass said.

"Daddy's not able to give us the whole story. We'll have to put the pieces together ourselves," Waylon said.

"Right now we have to focus on the most pressing problem, the psych evaluation," Thag said. "We can't let the judge find him competent to stand trial."

"Why don't you just put daddy on the stand when the time comes? Anybody who listens to him for two minutes would see that he has Alzheimer's, regardless of what some report says," Waylon said.

"If I put him on the stand, Rudd Brightwell, Jr. will eat

him alive. Plus there is no way for me to know what he would say once he starts talking. If he says anything about wanting to shoot someone, like he just did in the conference room, he will have cut his own throat. It's too dangerous a move," Thag said.

"What's our next move, then, counselor?" Reynolds said.

"The best way to discredit an expert's report is to discredit the expert," Thag said.

"Now you're talking my language," Waylon said. "I can pull up everything he's ever written, his school transcripts, his credit report. You name it. Maybe I can find something on him you can use."

"If you'll show me where to look, I'll help you search the records," Reynolds said. "How much time do we have, Thag?"

"You better get hopping. The competency hearing is at two o'clock tomorrow afternoon."

Waylon looked at his watch. It was ten minutes until four.

"I've got free high-speed Internet at the hotel," Shot Glass said.

"Looks like an all-nighter," Waylon said.

"I'll call around and see if any of the brethren in the criminal defense bar have run into Dr. Banks before. Meet me at my house at ten in the morning, and we'll go over whatever material you have been able to find," Thag said.

"We'll see you then. And thanks, Thag," Waylon said as he scrambled towards Reynolds' car.

Thag swung his feet into his Toyota and started the engine. He saw Reynolds and Waylon leave the parking lot ahead of him. As he drove toward home, one thought kept running through his head. Woody Wilson doesn't have a chance in hell.

Chapter 30

THAT NIGHT, WHILE his son and Shot Glass Reynolds tried to dig up dirt on Dr. Zebidiah Banks, while Odd Sheffield guarded him from above and while Theo Francis snored encouragement from his adjoining bunk where only a thin metal bar separated his head from Woody's feet, Woody dreamed and the shackles of his imprisonment, the dark coffin of his interment, slaked away and left him alone, alone on the water.

HE WAS FOURTEEN years old.

He and his dad stood in the metal shack in the backyard of his childhood home that his father called "the wood shop."

His father pointed at a pile of second hand lumber, planks of differing lengths, some almost new, others riddled with termite holes.

"If you want to build a boat, everything you need is right here," his dad said. He handed Woody a paperback book,

sweat-stained and lop eared, entitled 'How to Build a Skiff.'
"Follow the directions, and you'll be sea-worthy in no time."

His dad set up two saw horses on the floor near the wood pile, handed Woody a saw and returned to his lathe to put the finishing touches on a table leg.

Three months to the day later, on a January morning when the temperature dropped into the mid-twenties and the thin covering of a rare east Texas snow shower still splotched white the frozen ground, Woody finished the jon boat. He had tarred the joints with a large brush, then a smaller one, painted the vessel dark green, crafted two oars, all according to the directions from the book.

As his last act of preparedness, he cut a four foot length of lariat and tied a bowline knot in the steel eyelet he had secured to the bow. He wrapped the loose end of the rope around his gloved left hand and dragged the boat out the door of the wood shop, across the back yard, through scrub bush and over salamander holes until he reached the edge of the pond.

A patina of ice lay on the water closest to the shore as he turned the stern of the boat towards the lake and began to shove it away from land. He stepped in shallow holes that drenched his shoes and socks in icy water, but he kept pushing. At the last moment when the boat began to break free, he leaped forward, head first, into the ship. He lay motionless, face down, while the jon boat lilted. When he saw it wasn't going to sink, he rolled onto his back and sat up on the bench that spanned the middle of the skiff.

He positioned himself on the seat so that the boat floated level in the water, reached down and took the oars in his hands.

He made the oars his own as he worked them together, then one at a time, until he turned the bow towards the center of the pond. He glanced over his right shoulder, dipped both oars in the water and strained against them. A stiff north wind blew across the surface of the water and riddled it with miniature white caps. He stroked the oars in time with his breathing until he came to the point farthest from the shore. He lifted the oars from the water and laid them on the ribbed floor of the boat while he drifted. He turned his shoulders as far as he could from side to side to see the full surface of the pond. It looked to him like the Pacific Ocean.

After a few minutes, he stretched his feet in front of him, braced himself with his hands and lowered his back onto the floor of the boat. Thick clouds had gathered overhead. A wary hawk floated in circles above him as it cast its watchful gaze on the lake's recent interloper.

When the sleet started, he sat up and rowed back toward the spot where he launched the boat. As he neared the shore he looked over his shoulder one last time, judged the distance to his target and pulled with all his might against the hard water. When the boat jolted against solid ground, he brought the oars in, pushed himself to his feet, turned and darted for the bow. He grabbed the rope on his way past it and jumped as far as he could. When he hit the muddy ground his feet slogged in the mush, and he fell face first among the cattails. He got up, retrieved the end of the rope and yanked the jon boat until it cleared the water.

That was when he saw his dad.

"Not bad, skipper. Not bad at all," his dad said. "Mind if I give you a hand?"

His dad took the rope from Woody's hand and pulled

the boat while Woody went to the stern and pushed. When they got the boat to the back yard, they turned it upside down next to the south wall of the wood shop, and his dad brought a canvass tarp outside and covered it.

"You might want to wear some rubber boots next time," his dad said as he looked at Woody's wet, frozen feet. He reached out and mussed his son's hair, put his hands back in his coat pockets and walked towards the back door of the house.

"I think Momma has some hot chocolate on the stove," his dad said before he closed the door behind him.

HE AND MAGGIE were at St. Andrew Marina in Panama City when he spotted a "boat for sale" sign in a slip near the bait house.

"Let's take a look-see, baby," he said to Maggie.

"I'm with you, Captain Woody," she said.

The board walk led them to a twenty-eight foot Parker XLD with twin 200 outboards bolted to the transom. The steel bow railing shone in the summer sun, the fiberglass spotless as the boat bobbed in the water.

"She's a beaut'," Woody said.

Maggie nodded. "There's no telling how much trouble we could get in with a boat like that," Maggie said.

Woody grinned at her. "No telling," he said.

A man in shorts wearing a baseball cap and shirt with tropical flowers printed on it slung the cabin door open and walked out on deck. He had a cleaning bucket in one hand, a stiff-bristled brush in the other. He ran the brush over the vinyl seat covers and started to scrub the deck before he realized Woody and Maggie were watching him.

"Can I help you folks?" the man said.

"We're admiring your boat, captain. She looks like she could handle just about anything the sea might throw at her," Woody said.

"She's the toughest, best twenty-eight-footer afloat, if you ask me," he said. "I sure hate to part with her."

"Why would a man sell a boat like her?" Maggie asked.

"Divorce," the man on deck said. "I either have to sell her or live on her. I don't love her quite enough to make her my home."

"If we wanted to take her out for a test ride, what arrangement would you need?" Woody asked.

"You and the missus would have to watch your step as you came on board." The man walked to the starboard side of the boat next to where Maggie stood on the pier. He reached out his hand. She took it and stepped aboard. Then Woody hopped up on the gunwale, grabbed one of the steel handholds on the side of the cabin and stepped down on the deck.

"Make yourselves at home," the captain said.

Woody sat next to Maggie on an outside deck seat as the captain navigated the Parker out of the marina into St. Andrew Bay. When they cleared the no wake zone, the skipper revved the twin engines. The bow rose in the air and then dropped down as the boat came on plane. Maggie held on to her sun hat and Woody raised both his arms into the wind.

"It's like we're flying," Woody yelled at Maggie over the whining roar of the big engines.

The captain took them under the span of Hathaway Bridge into the waters of the Gulf Intracoastal Waterway before he turned the boat around and headed back toward the marina.

The sun was low in the sky, and dolphins swam along the port side. Maggie leaned her head on Woody's chest.

"We've got to have her," she whispered to Woody.

Woody didn't say anything, but he put his arm around her and pressed her tight against him for the remainder of the cruise.

At the dock, the captain helped them off the boat.

"What'd you think?" he asked.

"How much do you want for her?" Woody replied.

The captain gave him his asking price.

"Does that include the dolphins?" Maggie asked, leaning against his shoulder.

"I'll throw them in for free," he said.

"Then I guess we have a deal," Woody said. He shook hands with the captain. They discussed the closing on the boat as the captain walked them to their car. They shook hands again, and the captain started to walk away. He turned around for a second.

"Take good care of her," he said to Woody. He was looking at Maggie, not the Parker.

"Until the day I die," Woody said.

Woody and Maggie got in their car and drove through the marina parking lot.

"Let's swing by and see her one more time before we leave," Maggie said.

Woody made a u-turn and circled back to the closest vantage point he could find to their new boat. When they looked down at her, they saw the captain. He was on the pier next to the Parker. He leaned against her with both hands on her starboard bow. His chin dropped to his chest, and he began to cry.

Maggie rolled her window up and turned away from the sight. "Maybe we should come back another time," she said. She reached and took Woody's hand and held it in her lap the rest of the way home.

THE EARLY MORNING noises in the jail barracks began to rouse Woody. The mattress springs creaked as Odd Sheffield swung his feet over the side of the upper bunk.

"Let me take her out one more time," Woody said before he opened his eyes.

And God from above, in his implacable, inscrutable, mischievous wisdom, decided to grant Woody's last wish.

Chapter 31

ABOUT THREE O'CLOCK in the morning Waylon tried to make sense of what he and Shot Glass had learned after eight hours of Internet research.

"Dr. Zebidiah Banks is almost as invisible as Linus Schmutzer," he said. "I've found a couple of his reports, one You Tube video and little else."

Shot Glass chimed in. "I looked at the websites you gave me, but I didn't turn up a single lead," he said. "Let's see the video."

Waylon punched some keys on the keyboard, and in a minute, a video cued itself on the screen and asked permission to proceed.

"This can't be much," Waylon said. His face showed a solemn resignation.

When Waylon hit play on the video, the camera, probably from a smart phone in the gallery, zoomed in on a strange looking character, his black hair pulled tight in a ponytail, the skin on his face like stretched surgical gloves.

"I've seen a couple of pictures of him on the sites I looked at. That's him all right," Shot Glass said.

The video captured Zebidiah Banks on the witness stand somewhere in Florida under cross-examination. The defense attorney knew what he was doing.

"So, Dr. Banks, how many times have you testified in criminal cases in the state of Florida?" he asked.

"I would estimate about seventy-five," Banks said.

"And on how many of those occasions have you testified in favor of the State of Florida against the accused?" the defense attorney asked.

"All of them," Banks answered.

"So you always find the defendant competent to stand trial?"

"I always agree with the prosecution. Ninety-nine times out of a hundred, the suspects charged with the crime deserve to be in the penitentiary. Do you really think the motherfucker you represent, the sumbitch who committed aggravated sexual assault on an eleven-year-old girl, is not guilty, counselor?" Banks said.

The judge ruled Banks' testimony inadmissible in the case.

"This is great stuff. Burn it on a CD for Thag. He'll love it," Reynolds said.

The two cohorts crashed for three hours. At first light Shot Glass poked Waylon in the side to wake him, then walked to the sliding glass door on his balcony. He slid the door open and looked out at the ocean. He saw an oil tanker making its way along the shipping channel. Its skeleton crew manned the catwalks and shined flashlights to check for would-be pirates,

pirates that represented a real risk in the Indian Ocean, not the Gulf of Mexico.

For just a moment, Reynolds wondered what it would be like to be on a slow boat like that huge tanker. Like a prodigal son who cared not for his father's table, he had an ephemeral longing for a place where the foibles of his past didn't matter and the future was nothing more than a port with a strange name in a far country. He watched the ship until it receded on the horizon, lost in the morning mist where the ocean and the sky formed a seamless gray garment. He stepped off the balcony, closed the door and pulled the shade.

"Ready to head to Thag's place?" he said to Waylon.

"Give me fifteen minutes," Waylon said.

About seven o'clock they crossed the bridge at Destin Harbor as they drove east on Highway 98. A mile or so up the road they saw The Donut Hole restaurant on their left. Shot Glass turned into the parking lot.

"Since I stopped drinking whiskey, I like a good donut," he told Waylon.

The men sat down in a booth and waited for the waitress to bring their coffee.

"He's admitted he always testifies for the State. Shouldn't that be enough to establish that his testimony is tainted?" Waylon asked Reynolds.

"You'd think. But if the trial judge holds in favor of Rudd Brightwell, it will take Thag a while to get a reversal on appeal. In the meantime your dad will be locked up," Reynolds said. "And it's not often that an appeals court will overturn a trial judge's ruling on competence. The justices on the appeals court figure the judge who eyeballed the defendant is in a better position than they are to make that call. Plus, as a general rule, appeals court judges don't like criminal defendants anyway."

"I thought the system was supposed to be about justice," Waylon said.

"Welcome to the real world," Shot Glass said.

The waitress brought their donuts. Shot Glass dipped his in his coffee and plucked the shards that fell off the donuts out of the dark, hot liquid with a fork.

"Hey, it's better than being a drunk," he said to Waylon, who had watched his every move.

By the time they reached Clemon's house off the beach road in Seagrove Beach, Thag was pacing the floor. He had his court clothes on, a blue sports jacket that wouldn't button in the front, navy pants from the seventies with two inch cuffs, black patent leather penny loafers. His voice was stentorian, as if he were addressing a jury in closing argument.

"What do you have for me?" he said.

"Give it a break, Thag," Shot Glass said. "Wait 'til you see this."

Waylon set his laptop on top of a pile of papers on Thag's desk and played the You Tube video for him.

"Interesting," Thag said. "But it's probably not enough for Judge Moore to rule our way. He's a hardass sumbitch."

"It's all we could find," Waylon said. "Banks has made himself almost invisible."

"You could wonder why," Thag said. "Maybe he's smarter than we are. Let's go to the court house and take our positions. I'm ready to have a go at the mysterious Dr. Banks."

Waylon drove them to the courthouse in his 4 Runner. When they got to the courtroom on the third floor, they saw Maggie sitting on a bench in the foyer.

"How you doin', Momma?" Waylon said as he hugged her. Shot Glass and Thag shook her hand.

"This is a critical moment in Woody's case, Mrs. Wilson," Thag said.

"I understand, Mr. Clemons," she said.

"We are going to give it our best shot. But I am afraid the deck may be stacked against us," Thag said.

"The best you can do is all you can do," Maggie said.

They entered the courtroom at thirty-five minutes past one o'clock. Thag asked the clerk where they were on the docket. "You're the first case this afternoon, Mr. Clemons," she said.

Thag arranged five chairs around the defense counsel table, one each for him, Woody, Maggie, Waylon and Shot Glass. Maggie declined his offer.

"I'd rather be back here," she said as she sat down behind the railing in the front row of the gallery.

"Yes, ma'am," Thag said to her. "You're the boss."

Shot Glass came over to Thag.

"I'd rather be right here," he said as he sat down at the counsel table.

At fifty-eight minutes past one o'clock Rudd Brightwell, Jr. entered the courtroom from a side door, the door that led into Judge Moore's chambers. With him was the strange-looking man from the You Tube video, Dr. Zebidiah Banks.

Brightwell came over to Thag to shake hands before the hearing. Thag stood up, grabbed his hand and didn't let go.

"You been having a little picnic lunch with the judge, Rudd?"

Brightwell jerked his hand away from Thag's grip. "You

know me better than that, Thag," Rudd said as he sat down at the table for the counsel for the prosecution. Dr. Banks sat down beside him.

Thag knew that before Rudd Brightwell entered the courtroom he had engaged in what lawyers call an *ex parte* communication, a private conversation between the prosecutor and the presiding judge in a criminal case, a conversation in which the prosecutor made his case in the absence of the attorney for the accused. It was an unethical practice, a backroom tryst that tainted the legal system and produced not justice, but bias.

Shot Glass, a career cop, knew all about dirty tricks like *ex parte* communications. They were things that had created advantages for him for years. When he saw the exchange between Thag and Rudd, he knew he had found the right man to defend Woody Wilson.

And he knew they were going to lose.

"All rise. The honorable J.W. Moore presiding," the bailiff said as he pounded a gavel on a wooden pedestal.

Everyone in the courtroom stood up and waited for the judge to make his entrance. A door opened on the side of the courtroom and Judge Moore walked out.

His black robe shrouded his complicity with Rudd Brightwell, Jr.

"Where's Woody?" Thag asked. "He is supposed to be present for any hearing that implicates his freedom," he said to Reynolds.

Shot Glass shrugged he didn't know.

Judge Moore took the bench.

From the back of the courtroom, Deputy Bart walked down the center aisle until he came to the swinging half-door that separated the gallery from the pit where the lawyers would do battle. He stood at attention and wrung his hands.

"May I approach the bench, Your Honor?" he said. His voice, strained and unnatural, betrayed his nervousness.

Judge Moore looked up from the papers he was reviewing before the hearing started. He didn't like anything that was unscripted.

"Come forward, Deputy Bartholomew," he said.

Thag knew something was up.

Judge Moore rolled his chair to the side of the bench closest to his clerk and motioned for Deputy Bart to come around. The two spoke in tones so low that no one else in the courtroom could make out the subject of the conversation.

"Will the District Attorney approach the bench?" Judge Moore said. The skin had tightened on his face.

Thag watched while the judge and the DA exchanged words. Deputy Bart stood at attention next to Rudd and said nothing. When Moore finished with Brightwell, the DA grabbed Bart's right arm with his hand and escorted him to a far corner of the courtroom.

Everyone watched as the DA spoke to the deputy and stuck him in the chest with his index finger like a football coach confronting a running back after a fumble. Deputy Bart still said nothing. When the conversation ended, the deputy marched out the back of the courtroom and shut the door.

Finally Judge Moore made his pronouncement.

"In the matter of the State of Florida versus Woodrow Wilson, the hearing scheduled for two o'clock has been canceled until further notice from the Court," Judge Moore said.

The judge stood up and began to walk out of the courtroom.

Thag shot to his feet.

"Your Honor, Pythagoras Clemons for the defense. We have our witnesses here and are prepared to move forward. We object to the Court canceling the hearing at the last minute."

"You may be ready, Thag," Judge Moore said. "But your client isn't."

"What do you mean, Your Honor?" Thag asked.

"The sheriff's office has just informed me that Woodrow Wilson and two other inmates escaped from custody about fifteen minutes ago."

"What?" Maggie said when she heard the word *escaped*. She jumped to her feet. "What have they done to Woody?" she cried out.

Moore slammed his gavel on the bench.

"Please sit down, ma'am," he said to Maggie. "I will not tolerate any outbursts in my court."

Maggie sat down and grabbed the arms of her seat with both hands. Waylon got up from his chair at the counsel table, walked through the swinging door and sat down next to his mother. He put his left arm around her shoulders and held her.

Judge Moore continued. "The sheriff's department has a manhunt underway for the escapees. When they return them to custody, we'll proceed with the competency hearing. Until then, Court is adjourned."

Moore stepped down from the bench, opened the door to his chambers and left the courtroom.

Rudd moved next to Thag.

"I've never known an incompetent prisoner who could stage a jailbreak, Thag. When we get Woody Wilson, I'm going to fry his ass."

Rudd and Banks picked up their case folders and filed

passed the men at the defense table. When Banks caught Shot Glass studying the pale skin of his face, he winked at him, turned his back and walked out of the courtroom.

"What a prick," Shot Glass said as he saw the door shut behind Dr. Banks.

In the lobby, Rudd pulled out his cell phone and placed a call to the sheriff. Dr. Banks waved goodbye to the DA and rode the elevator to the ground floor. He walked to his car and got out the cell phone he had stashed in the center console. He hit a number on speed dial.

When a voice came on the line, Banks said, "All aboard?"

"All aboard," the person on the other end of the call said.

Banks hung up the phone, turned it off and pulled out of the parking lot. He drove by the jail on his way out of town. When he saw the bars on the windows, he grinned.

"I love it when a plan comes together, Captain Woody," he said.

Chapter 32

AN HOUR LATER, Waylon and his mother had retired to Maggie's condo to await word on the jailbreak. Meanwhile Shot Glass did what he did best. He investigated a crime.

He drove to the site where the escapees were last seen, parked next to a marked Walton County Sheriff's Office patrol unit with the words "Chief Deputy" painted on the driver's door in black capital letters, got out and approached the man who appeared to be in charge.

In Reynolds' experience, the chief deputy was the old head guy who ran the sheriff's office while the sheriff ass-kissed politicians, gave speeches and accepted bribes. If a chief deputy wasn't corrupt, he was corruptible.

The chief deputy was a uniformed red-faced officer in his early sixties with faded brown hair and a pot belly. He had weary eyes and fingers that had grown so fat his wedding ring looked like the neck band on a prize county fair FFA rooster.

Reynolds flashed his special investigator badge.

"How'd it go down?" he asked without any introductions.

The chief deputy looked at him.

"Chief Deputy Sammy Arceneau," he said as he stuck his hand out to Shot Glass. "I guess you must be Shot Glass Reynolds."

Reynolds shook his hand and gave him a two finger *what the hell* salute.

"I'm not quite sure whose side you are on in this case, Reynolds?" Arceneau said.

"The side of truth and justice, as always," Reynolds said.

"That doesn't tell me much," the chief said.

"It's hard to figure sometimes," Reynolds said.

They were standing in the parking lot of Moe's convenience store. Deputies had shut it down for the duration of the investigation.

Moe was short for Mohammed.

The manager of the store, an Asian import who spoke like a comedian doing a bad Indian accent, came up to the chief deputy.

"I know nothing about this. I have to open the store. This is costing me much money," he said.

The chief ignored him while he explained to Shot Glass what he knew.

He spoke police-ese, the language he would use when he wrote his report.

"Deputy Bart took six trustees out on a work detail earlier today. They were supposed to pick up trash along the road so things would look ..."

He paused for a minute as he searched for the right word. "*appropriate* when the governor comes to town next week on an official visit."

Shot Glass glanced and saw trash bags, half-full, abandoned along both sides of the road.

"Wilson and two other prisoners named Odessa Sheffield and Theophilus Francis were working the stretch of highway closest to Moe's. The three other trustees were further up the road," the chief said.

"Odd and Theo," Reynolds said under his breath.

"What did you say?"

"Nothing."

"Bart got a call on his cell from someone complaining that the guys down the road were making lewd comments at passing motorists, so he left Wilson and the others that were on this end of the detail and walked to the other three to straighten them out. When he got all the way up there," the deputy pointed to a spot a couple of hundred yards from Shot Glass and him, "he looked back this direction and saw Wilson, Sheffield and Theophilus piling into a white van. He yelled for them to stop, but the van took off. The last time Bart saw the van, it turned right, that is to the north, at the first street that intersected the road."

Shot Glass thought about the sequence of events.

"Did Deputy Bart get much of a look at the driver?" he asked.

"He said he couldn't be sure, but he thought it was a black female."

"Were either of the trustees with Wilson black?"

"Odessa Sheffield. I've sent officers to his last known address to see if they can find a wife or girlfriend."

"Not likely, Chief," Shot Glass said. "If she was in on it, she's long gone by now. Any hits on the van?"

"We have every road in this part of the county shut down.

We're stopping every vehicle that is a close match to the van."

The chief's cell phone rang. He took it out of its belt holster and answered.

"Yeah. OK," he said to the caller before he hung up. "Shit," he said as he looked at the "beer for sale" signs taped to the windows of the convenience store.

Shot Glass waited.

"They just found a van matching the description of the suspect vehicle in the Publix parking lot on Highway 98. No sign of the escapees," the chief said. "They ran the plates on the van. When they called the owner in Navarre Beach, he told them it had been stolen sometime during the night last night. Navarre Beach PD confirmed the stolen vehicle report."

"So right now you ain't got shit," Shot Glass said.

"Bingo."

"Thanks, Chief," Shot Glass said. "I thlnk I get the picture."

"What picture?" The chief had heard that Reynolds had a sixth sense about these things.

"It's a snatch and grab. Odd Sheffield was the mastermind. Woody probably didn't know anything about it before the deal went down."

"What about Francis?" the chief asked.

"I've seen a million like him. He's just a stupid kid who thought a jailbreak would look good on his record, make him look like a tough guy. He's too young and ignorant to understand the grief he just bought himself."

The chief thought about what Reynolds said.

"I know that kid's momma. He's been a handful since the day he was born. I doubt he realizes he just turned his misdemeanor arrest for smoking pot into a potential life sentence."

"I guess most of us don't know how bad we have fucked up until later," Shot Glass said.

"I know I didn't," the chief said.

The chief shook hands with Reynolds and walked to his patrol car. Reynolds saw him take a clipboard off the dash, lay it on the hood of his car and start writing his preliminary report. After he wrote a couple of sentences, he put his Bic pen down and called someone on his cell. He rested his gut on the side of the car as he talked. The call lasted about a minute.

Shot Glass figured he had called Theo Francis' mother. He also figured the chief knew her a lot better than he had allowed.

After the chief ended the call, he wrote a few more sentences on the form on his clipboard and tossed it in the front seat of his car. He glanced up and turned around to Shot Glass who hadn't moved.

"One more thing, Reynolds," he said.

"Sure, Chief."

"You have any idea where they are going?

"My guess is that it has something to do with a boat," Shot Glass said. He had heard Waylon's stories about Woody's love of the sea.

The chief shook his head. "You have any idea how many boats there are between Pensacola and Apalachicola?" the chief said.

"That's probably why it's a pretty good plan," Reynolds said.

Chapter 33

THE NEXT MORNING at the condo, Waylon got up at sunrise. When he walked into the breakfast room, Maggie was already sitting at the table with a cup of coffee. Waylon walked over to her, leaned down and gave her hug around the neck.

"No word, yet," she said.

"Since they didn't catch them yesterday with all the road blocks set up, I bet they could be anywhere by now," Waylon said.

"Shot Glass thinks they have headed for a boat somewhere, but Panama City has all the marinas under surveillance without any sightings. He also thinks Odd Sheffield is behind the whole thing."

"Things have gone from bad to worse, I'm afraid. Thag says even if your dad could have beaten the charges against him from the Tom Thumb situation, he won't stand a chance on the escape count," Maggie said. "I never thought our lives would play out like this at the end."

Waylon sat down across from his mom and took her hands in his. "It's not over yet, Momma. When the truth comes out, everyone will see that dad was just in the wrong place at the wrong time. He probably didn't even know what was coming down. I bet he thought he had permission to get in that van."

Maggie didn't say anything. She looked out the window at the Gulf of Mexico. To the east, storm clouds roiled in the sky. The breeze freshened and kicked up three-foot waves that crashed just short of the beach. She could see the top of the red flag that warned people on the beach that the water was too dangerous for swimming.

"You want to see if the paper is here, yet, Hon?" she said to Waylon. "I'd like to see if there is anything in it we haven't heard yet about the jailbreak."

Waylon got up and went to the front door. He looked out the window at the elevator lobby where the paper boy threw the morning paper. He saw it near the front door mat. When he opened the door, it snagged on a large manila envelope. Waylon picked it and the newspaper up and went back to the kitchen table. He handed Maggie the paper.

"What's that?" she said when she saw the envelope.

"I don't know. It was by the door," Waylon said.

The envelope had no writing on it. He took his pocket knife and slit the top, felt inside. He reached his hand in and pulled out the contents. There was a cover sheet with handwriting on it.

He read the note out loud to Maggie. "For the good times," it said. It wasn't signed or dated.

When he slid the paper to the side, they saw an 8 x10 glossy black and white photo. Waylon pushed it close to

Maggie so they could study it together. In the picture, a young boy beams with pride as he holds a fish up in the air. He is standing on the deck of a boat next to a man who wears a smile so wide it looks as if his face might break.

They recognized it immediately. Maggie pushed her chair back and rushed into the master bedroom. In a second, she came back with a framed print of the same picture.

"It's the one he had behind his desk at the post office," Maggie said.

"The one from the trip he and I took together that time. He hailed a captain that was passing by and had him take the picture," Waylon said.

Maggie thought about that trip. Woody had told her about it a thousand times.

"He sent a copy of that picture to the captain who took the shot," Maggie said. "Woody kept up with him off and on through the years. I think they even went fishing together once."

She looked at Waylon.

"Where were you when you caught that big grouper?"

Waylon understood why she asked.

"The more important question is probably where that captain called home port," Waylon said. He turned the picture over. On the back in Woody's handwriting appeared the captain's name and an address near Point Washington.

"A boat could put in there, intersect the Intracoastal and go anywhere it wanted in the eastern half of North America," Maggie said. "Woody and I talked about making that trip. They call it the Great Loop. There are even people who call themselves *loopers* who spend years on those waterways."

"Where's the *Miss Maggie* now, Momma?" Waylon asked.

"So far as I know, it is still at the slip at St. Andrew Marina, but I haven't been over there to check on it in several weeks."

"Write the slip number down for me," Waylon said. He called Shot Glass on his cell.

"Can you check out a lead for me?" he said when Reynolds answered.

"Fire away," he said.

He read the slip number off the paper.

"It's at St. Andrew Marina in Panama City," Waylon said.

"The Panama City PD is all over that place. I'm sure they have already checked it," Shot Glass said.

"They probably didn't know where to look. Daddy swapped slips with one of the guys a few years back and they never did any paper work on it. For sentimental reasons, he wanted the original slip where the boat was when he and momma bought it. If the police are watching the slip they think is his, they're looking in the wrong spot."

"I'll call you back," Reynolds said.

About thirty minutes later, Waylon's cell rang.

"The cops are hovered on the south end of the marina. The slip number you gave me is on the north east side nearest the road. It's empty," Shot Glass said.

"That's what I thought," Waylon said. "Swing by the condo and pick me up. I think I know where daddy is."

"I'm on my way," Reynolds said.

Before he hung up, Waylon added one more comment. "And you might want to bring your gun."

"I never leave home without it," Reynolds said as he ended the call, stuck a flashing emergency light on the top of his car and raced towards Seagrove Beach.

Chapter 34

ODD SHEFFIELD DITCHED the dark blue '89 Nissan Sentra his girl friend had provided the jail-breakers as a get-away car in the woods just east of Eden Gardens State Park at one-thirty in the morning while Waylon and Maggie slept, and while the Walton County Sheriff's office searched people on the bridges that filtered tourists off the island.

He pulled a prepaid cell phone from his shirt pocket and dialed his girl friend. The call went to voice mail on the first ring.

"It's been fun, baby. Now take the money and run," he said. He ended the call and got out of the car, hurled the phone into the brackish water of the bay.

He opened the passenger side back door of the car where the other occupants lay on the floor board.

"Time to hoof it, Mr. Woody," he said. "The Germans will overrun our position in the next few minutes."

Theo Francis looked at Odd.

He wondered what the fuck he meant.

"The Battle of the Bulge," Sheffield said to him. "Remember?"

"Oh, yeah," Francis said. He acted like he understood. He didn't have a clue.

"Just wake up Mr. Woody and follow me," Sheffield said. "That is unless you want to spend the rest of your life in the pen."

Theo shook Woody hard.

"We gotta move right now, Mr. Woody," he said. "They're almost on top of us."

Woody opened his eyes. He didn't say anything, but he nodded at Francis and rolled out of the car onto the wet dirt of the boggy wood. He picked himself up and fell in behind Odd.

"Where are we going, Odd?" he whispered.

"Stay low, Mr. Woody. There's a place around the bend where GIs are welcome any hour of the night," Sheffield said.

The three men trudged through the undergrowth. They followed a blacktop one lane county road as it weaved along the high ground next to a bayou. They soon came to a house that looked deserted. It was a faux New England cottage, a couple of years old. A story and half tall, it had a small pool and an elevated board walk that led a hundred yards behind the house across a swamp to a covered boat slip on a narrow creek that drained into Choctawhatchee Bay.

Odd felt around in the dark near the back door.

"Got it," he said as he held up a key. He inserted it into the back door lock and pushed the door open. He motioned the men inside. "Don't turn on any lights," he said.

The men felt their way through the house. It was fully furnished and clean.

"Are you sure nobody's home?" Theo said. "I don't want to get shot."

"We're invited," Odd said. "We have the place to ourselves 'til mid-morning tomorrow."

Odd went to a closet next to the pantry in the kitchen. He opened the door and felt around until he pulled out three garbage bags. Each bag had a gray duct tape label with a name on it.

"There are some street clothes in here that ought to fit. Get rid of that orange jumpsuit," he said to Francis.

Theo took the bag with his name on it, fished out some camo gear and changed clothes. He put his jail clothes in the bag and put it back in the closet.

"What happens tomorrow morning?" he asked Odd.

"We are on our way," Sheffield said.

He turned to Woody who had hunkered down in a corner next to a window.

Woody raised his head and peered outside every couple of minutes.

"We're safe here, Mr. Woody. You should get some sleep. At first light, someone will be here to pick us up," Odd said.

"Where's Maggie? I thought you said she would be waiting for me here," Woody said. He had no idea where he was or why he was there. "Deputy Bart is probably worried sick about us by now."

"Maggie will be with the rescue detail. You'll see her first thing in the morning. Deputy Bart is the one who arranged this place for us. Don't worry, Mr. Woody. Everything is going to be all right," Sheffield said.

Woody calmed down and soon fell asleep.

"It's not right to lie to the old man like that," Francis said. "It's not going to be all right for any of us, and you know it. I say we leave him here and hightail it. Someone will find him in a day or two and get him some help. We can be in North Carolina or South Padre Island by then."

"Doing what? Don't you reckon the two of us might stick out like sore thumbs if we stopped at the Waffle House?" Sheffield said. "We're all in this together. We follow the doc's plan. It's worked to a T so far."

Theo grabbed Sheffield's shirt with both hands.

"I don't trust that crazy shrink. He may be all we have right now, but if I get the chance, I'm bailing. I don't plan to spend the rest of my life in lock up for the sake of Mr. Woody."

"I hear you, kid. But there ain't no way out. You're in or you're not. If you want to run, you'd better do it now. By tomorrow your chance to leave will be gone."

Francis started toward the door. He stopped and sat down in the middle of the dark living room.

"I just smoked a little weed. That's all," he said and he started to cry.

Sheffield went over to him. "First you do one thing wrong, then another," he said. "You wake up one day and all you have in front or behind you are bad decisions made or about to be made. There's no way out. Get your arms around it. It's how things shook out for us."

"So what the fuck are we doing?" Francis said.

"We're trying to do at least one thing right in our sorry lives," Sheffield said.

"What's that?" Francis asked.

"We're going to see that Woody Wilson gets a fair shake," Odd said.

Theo Francis looked at Woody asleep on the polished pine floor. In the dim light of the room, he crawled to the couch, found a wool blanket. He took it to Woody and draped it over him.

"Okay. I guess that's something," he said.

Chapter 35

A **FEW MINUTES** before eight o'clock Waylon's cell rang again.

"I'm in the parking lot," Reynolds said.

"I'll be right down there," Waylon said.

Shot Glass got out of his car, leaned against the hood and waited. In a minute he saw Waylon and Maggie on the fourth floor landing by the elevator. Maggie went to the railing and waved at Reynolds.

"Be careful, Sherwood," she said.

"Always, Maggie," he said.

She hugged Waylon's neck before he jumped on the elevator. "Bring your dad home to me," she said as the door closed.

Waylon got in the car with Shot Glass.

He had already programmed the address from the back of the photo into his handheld GPS unit. When they got to the street, Waylon gave him the directions. "Turn left. When you get to 395, take a right and follow the road north to Point

Washington. It's only about three miles." He looked straight ahead.

"Kind of on edge, are we?" Reynolds said.

"Sorry. I'm not used to life and death situations, jail breaks and stuff like that," Waylon said.

"Me either," Reynolds said.

Waylon looked down at the center console and saw a semi-automatic handgun.

"That's not what you usually carry is it?" he asked.

"No. That's a Kimber TLE Two .45-caliber. It's what the LA SWAT team uses. It's not a subtle gun. In a circumstance like this, a man needs a pair and a spare."

He pulled his windbreaker open with his right hand so that Waylon could see his Smith and Wesson Model 686 .357-caliber revolver in his shoulder holster. He reached down and patted the inside of his left ankle, too, where he had another pistol concealed.

"Did I ever tell you how I got the nickname *Shot Glass*?" Reynolds asked while he drove.

"I thought it was pretty obvious," Waylon said.

"Yes and no. So far as I know, I am the only guy who can draw a revolver and hit two shot glasses in mid air," Reynolds said.

"Sounds like you have some experience at it."

"It used to happen about once a week in a different bar somewhere in Nashville. It's the sort of thing a police detective shouldn't do if he hopes to advance in the department."

"I take it you emptied some high octane liquid from the shot glasses before they became air borne," Waylon said.

"That was a mandatory element of the trick-shooting exhibition."

They crossed over Highway 98 and drove about a mile north before they came to the old, white Methodist church with a cemetery next to it where Maggie's parents were buried.

"According to the GPS, the address is due east of us, about five hundred yards," Waylon said. "There is a bayou on the back side of the house and only one way in and out by car."

"I doubt they are expecting us," Reynolds said. "Whoever tipped you off probably didn't let them in on that part of the deal. I say we get as close as we can by car, then we'll hike the last stretch."

"What do we do when we find them?"

"We'll have to make that part up as we go. There's a good chance they are gone already. If we find them and it is just your dad, Odd Sheffield and Theo, I don't expect much resistance."

"You say that like you are expecting someone else to join them," Waylon said.

"I am," Reynolds said. "That's why I packed so much heat. If the shooting starts, try to get yourself and Woody out of the line of fire. Stay down until I give you the all clear signal."

"What's the signal?"

"I'll yell 'all clear' as loud as I can," Reynolds said.

"Figures," Waylon said.

In the cottage, the fugitives slept until seven thirty. Odd woke Francis. He went to the front bedroom window and looked outside.

"Looks like the coast is clear," he told Theo. "There are some ham sandwiches in the fridge."

He went to Woody who was curled in a fetal position on the floor. His mouth was open, and his eyes twitched like he was dreaming.

"Mr. Woody. Mr. Woody," he said as he nudged him gently with his hand. "Mr. Woody, it's time to get up. We're going fishing today."

When Sheffield said the word *fishing*, Woody opened his eyes. "We're going fishing?" he said.

"Yes, sir. You reckon you can find us a honey hole?"

"If there's one out there, I can find it," Woody said. He stretched himself and hopped to his feet. He had on his new camo outfit.

Odd looked at Francis. "I changed him into those clothes before I went to sleep last night," he said. "I thought it might make things go a little smoother for him this morning."

"Some hardened criminal you are," Odd said.

"Ready to catch some fish, Francis?" Woody said as he patted Theo on the back. "I'll need a first mate."

"I'm your man, Captain Woody," Theo said.

REYNOLDS LIFTED A pair of binoculars to his face and studied the cottage from a grove of pine trees in a bog thirty yards south of the house.

"I can see some movement inside. Let's wait a while and see who comes out," he said. He handed the field glasses to Waylon who checked out the location.

"There is a long board walk that leads to the slip on the creek. I can see a boat that looks like the *Miss Maggie* tied up there," Waylon said.

"The *Miss Maggie*?" Shot Glass said.

"That's daddy's boat. What happens if they make a break for it out the back and head for the boat?"

"We run like hell and hope we can catch them before the ship leaves. Then I'll use my finely honed negotiating skills to detain them while we devise the rest of the plan," Reynolds said.

"You're not going to arrest them?" Waylon said.

"It may come to that, but I hope not. I want to explore some other options first if I can," Reynolds said.

"They're on the move," Waylon said as he pointed toward the board walk.

The three escapees walked out the back door. Woody was in the lead, his gaze focused on the planks of the walk, his gait steady. Behind him, Odd and Theo had a hand on handles on the opposite ends of an orange Bass Pro Shop ice chest. The cooler hung low and heavy between them as they waddled toward the Parker. They were in no hurry. They were just some guys looking forward to a day on the water.

"I only see three. How about you?" Waylon said.

"Ditto," Reynolds said. "Let's go."

BY THE TIME that Shot Glass and Waylon set foot on the board walk, the escapees had reached the boat slip.

"Keep your eyes open," Reynolds said.

They caught their breath and started walking toward the three men.

"Ahoy mates," Shot Glass yelled half way down the walk.

The men looked up at them for a second, then turned back to loading the ice chest in the boat.

About ten yards from the Parker, Waylon got a better look at the boat. Someone had covered the name *Miss Maggie* with tape; painted over it was a new name for the vessel, *Nothing Left to Lose*. He saw a small rowboat tied to the outside of the slip.

He tugged on Reynolds' jacket.

"Do you see that?" he asked.

"What?"

"The skiff tied up on the far side of the dock."

Reynolds squinted.

"I see it," he said.

"Daddy built that boat when he was a kid. It's been in our family my whole life. The name on the Parker is changed, too. Someone has gone to a lot of trouble to set up this deal," Waylon said.

"I thought so," Shot Glass said.

When they reached the boat, Waylon and Reynolds stood on the pier. Shot Glass pulled his revolver and let it hang in his hand next to his right leg.

"Police," he said. "Come out with your hands above your heads."

The three men had entered the cabin. They didn't come out. "I said show yourselves now," Reynolds called out.

Woody stepped out of the cabin and faced Reynolds. He grinned when he saw him and showed no sign that he understood his situation. "We're going fishing," Woody said. "Y'all want to join us?"

"How many crew members do you have, captain?" Reynolds asked.

"Just me, Theo and Odd," he said. "But that's enough for a short cruise."

"Where are they?"

"Down below," Woody said. "I'll get 'em."

"Our guests are here," Woody said as he opened the cabin door and yelled inside.

In a minute, the other two men came out of the cabin and stepped onto the deck. Odd acted as the spokesman.

"We thought Mr. Woody would enjoy one more turn on the water," he said to Waylon and Reynolds. "So we brought him here."

Reynolds assessed the scene.

"You and who else?" he said.

As if on cue, the cabin door opened again. A strange looking man with a black ponytail tied in a rubber band came out. His face was pale and looked like off-white latex.

"I'm the *who else*," the man said.

He held an AK 47 in his hands. He pointed it at Reynolds. When Odd and Theo saw the assault rifle, they backed up against the cabin.

"Hold on, doc," Theo said. "We didn't know anything about any guns."

Banks looked at Odd and Francis. He didn't say anything.

"It's good to see you again, Dr. Banks," Reynolds said. With his right thumb he cocked the hammer on the Smith and Wesson. All the men heard it click into firing position. Reynolds knew there was a pretty good chance he could get one round off before Banks opened up, if Shot Glass was prepared to trade his life for that of the psychiatrist.

"I don't think we have to resort to violence to resolve the issues between us, Detective Reynolds. I would like to propose an alternate plan," Banks said.

"I generally like an option that doesn't include me getting killed or having to kill someone else," Reynolds said. The tip of his trigger finger edged towards the trigger.

Waylon hadn't moved since Banks stepped out of the cabin. He felt like his feet were frozen to the pier. He was fighting the urge to pee on himself.

"Captain Woody would like to take us out for a day on the water. I know a spot where we are almost sure to make a catch that we will never forget. My proposition is simple. Waylon and you join us on board; we enjoy the cruise together, maybe even get to know each other in the process. When we finish our expedition, we'll come back here and you will be free to take any steps you see fit in regard to any of us. In the meantime, both of you," he looked at Waylon for a second, "agree not to contact the authorities or anyone else unless an emergency arises."

"Are you expecting one to arise?" Reynolds asked.

"Perhaps," Banks said.

Reynolds thought it over.

"And what about all these guns?" he said.

"I will stow mine away if you will do the same. But we agree to keep them handy just in case we have to defend ourselves against an external threat."

"Do you expect us to encounter one?" Reynolds said.

"Perhaps," Banks said.

Shot Glass looked at Waylon. The color had drained from his face. He had his gaze on Woody.

"Deal," Reynolds said. "You put your gun down first."

"I sense that there is still a certain element of distrust between us," Banks said. "Allow me to demonstrate my good faith."

"Be my guest," Shot Glass said.

Banks let the tip of the rifle barrel dip so that it pointed at the deck. He walked to a wooden foot locker, lifted the lid and placed the AK 47 inside it. He flipped the latch to the footlocker closed, slipped a padlock through the latch and locked it.

He took the key to the pad lock from his coat pocket and dropped it in the ice chest.

"Your turn," he said to Reynolds. He kicked a plastic case with his left shoe. The case was just the right size for three pistols.

Shot Glass put his thumb on the hammer of the .357 and eased it against the firing pin. He holstered it and stepped down into the boat. He put the revolver in the case, reached behind him and drew the Kimber from his waist band and laid it in the case next to the revolver. Then he knelt on his right knee, pulled up his left pants' leg and removed a light weight .38 revolver with a two-inch barrel. He placed it in the box next to the other pistols. He closed the lid on the box and snapped it tight.

Reynolds looked at Waylon, who still stood on the pier. "You coming with us?" he said.

Waylon stepped down into the boat.

"While we're at it, we might as well get rid of these, too, for the duration of our voyage," Banks said. He took his cell phone out of his shirt pocket and dropped it in a canvass bag. He held the bag in front of Reynolds, then Waylon, who placed their cell phones in the bag. Banks walked to the cabin, opened a door on a cabinet and stuffed the bag inside. He returned to face Reynolds.

"That wasn't so bad, was it?" Banks said to Shot Glass. "Now that we are all aboard, I think I can get rid of this, too."

Banks took his left hand and grabbed his hair at the point where it joined the top of his forehead. He yanked hard and the black wig came off. He tossed it in the brackish water near the shore where it floated for a second before it got caught in the brush.

Then Banks placed both hands around the base of his own neck, pressed his thumbs against the skin to get a good grip and peeled the latex covering off his face. He threw it into the water beside the wig and then ran his fingers through his hair to smooth it.

"What the hell?" Odd Sheffield said.

The man Sheffield knew as Dr. Banks walked over to him and shook his hand. "Allow me to introduce myself. My name is Linus Schmutzer, the second. Most of my patients just call me Doc Smooth."

"Don't worry," Woody said to Odd. "Me and Doc Smooth go way back. Don't we, Doc?"

"Way back, Captain Woody," Schmutzer said.

"If you don't mind, I'll just call you Linus," Shot Glass said.

Linus looked at Reynolds. "Suit yourself, Detective Reynolds."

"Is everybody ready to go fishing?" Woody said.

The men nodded and began to mill around the deck of the boat.

"Cast those lines off and let's get underway," Woody said to Theo.

"Aye, aye, Captain Woody," Theo said as he set the boat free from the pier.

Woody backed her out of the slip and into the creek channel. "Where are we headed, Doc Smooth?" Woody yelled through the cabin door.

Schmutzer entered the cabin and pointed at a GPS he had mounted on the instrument panel.

"Follow that arrow, Captain Woody. It will lead us right where we need to go. If we want to catch the conditions when they are just right, we'll have to make pretty good time."

"Hold on to your hats, then," Woody said.

He moved the throttle forward, and the twin engines came to life. Woody followed the creek channel until the water widened into Choctawhatchee Bay. When he saw the markers to the Intracoastal, he turned east. He pushed the lever hard forward and the engines roared as their propellers churned through the waterway.

"Yippee," Woody said as he turned to look at the men on deck. "We're flying, boys. We're flying."

Chapter 36

WOODY TOOK THE Gulf Intracoastal Waterway through the Canyon, the deep cut the Army Corps of Engineers had dug to connect Choctawhatchee Bay with West Bay near Panama City.

Ospreys perched in the high branches of the trees, miniature bald eagles surveying their dominion.

Except for occasional pleasure crafts that met them on their way to the east pass into the Gulf at Destin Harbor, the men had the water to themselves. As the sun rose higher, the temperature on the late October day climbed to the high sixties. The Canyon sheltered them from the slight south breeze. Had the *Nothing Left To Lose* been a sailing vessel, it would have been becalmed, stranded in a placid expanse of salt water.

Woody watched the rpm gauge on the engines and settled into the most efficient speed where the motors exerted the least effort to drive the ship forward. He cut the engines back when he came close to another boat to reduce his wake.

He scanned the water moment by moment and kept his right hand on the wheel as he made minor adjustments to course.

Waylon entered the cabin and took a seat on the captain's chair next to Woody. He watched his dad and marveled at the precision of his movements, his total control of the heavy boat.

"You make it look as easy as falling off a horse, Captain Woody," he said after a while.

Woody grinned at him. "There's never a bad day on the water, son," he said.

Waylon thought he caught just a glimmer of recognition in Woody's eyes.

"No, sir. At least I've never had one," he said.

"Ever do any fishing around here, my friend?" Woody asked. Now Waylon knew Woody couldn't come up with his name.

"My dad and I trolled up and down here a lot when I was younger. The times I spent on the salt with him were the best ones of my life," Waylon said.

"You're a lucky man to have a father like that, son. My dad taught me to love the water, too. He made me build my own boat when I was a kid. She's still as seaworthy as the first day I took her out."

"I'll bet she'll last a hundred years, Captain Woody," Waylon said.

"I hope so, son. I'd like my boy to have her one day."

I bet when the time comes, he'll love her as much as you have," Waylon said. He slid off the seat, patted Woody on the back and stepped towards the cabin door.

"Let me know when you're ready to put a line in the water," Woody said.

"I'll let you know." Waylon walked out on deck, made his way to the bow and sat down. He hung his feet over the side of the boat, grabbed the railing, closed his eyes and felt the wind on his face. He turned his head to the right far enough to see Woody at the wheel. He was singing an old tune made popular an eternity ago by the Sons of the Pioneers.

Waylon joined in. "Lonely but free I'll be found, drifting along with the tumbling tumbleweeds."

In his heart Waylon knew this was it: the last time, the last day of Woody's seventy years on the water.

And he thanked God that he was with him on the *Nothing Left To Lose*.

Chapter 37

AS THE BOAT approached Hathaway Bridge in Panama City, Shot Glass strolled across the deck and sat down next to Linus Schmutzer. He leaned forward, rested his elbows on his knees and looked hard at a dark spot as it spread on the white fiberglass deck. He didn't turn his head when he spoke.

"This is the way I have it figured. Your old man and your uncle had some kind of deal that involved Woody. Somewhere along the way, you became a beneficiary of the agreement. You could care less for most people; you may even hate them. But Woody got under your skin, and you couldn't shake him, even when you knew your dad and your uncle weren't going to be around to enforce your obligation to him. So you put together a plan that you thought would give Woody a little peace at the end of his life. When Woody escaped from you, he threw a kink in the original plan, but you improvised and came up with this one.

"How am I doing so far?" Shot Glass said.

"Impressive, if somewhat flawed," Schmutzer said. "Please continue."

"I figure you're not the sort of guy to leave many loose ends, so you have a few other things up your sleeve. For sure, you have no intention of turning yourself in to me at the end of this voyage," Shot Glass said.

"Makes sense," Schmutzer said.

Reynolds continued. "There are a few gaps in my theory, like why did you have to kill Dr. Davis?"

"Who said I did?" Linus said.

At that remark, Reynolds turned and looked Schmutzer in the eye. "I'm sure you did it. I just don't know why yet."

"Suppose the autopsy shows he was terminal with cancer and may have decided he didn't want to go that way. Maybe he saw his death as an opportunity of some sort to do a little good on his way out of this life," Linus said.

Reynolds thought about it. "Maybe, but I doubt it. I think you wanted him out of your way so you could be in Nashville in time to intersect with Woody. A position at a mental hospital formed a good cover for you."

"You're a very cynical man, Reynolds," Schmutzer said.

"Comes with the territory," Shot Glass said.

Reynolds wasn't finished. "And what's with the masquerade about Dr. Banks? You wrote a report that you knew would keep Woody in jail and send him to trial, while at the same time you plotted the jail break. Why didn't you say he was incompetent, have him sent to a psychiatric unit and spring him there?"

"Maybe I needed a little time to put a plan together and some inside help to pull it off." Linus cast a glance at Sheffield and Francis. "Woody wasn't the only prisoner I evaluated. Odd has been mentally unbalanced ever since he came home from Vietnam."

Shot Glass looked at Sheffield for a minute.

"Plus, I figured it was just a matter of time before you would uncover my true identity and expose me. I couldn't let that happen in the middle of a competency hearing. It might have been the first time the testifying psychiatrist at such a hearing became a detainee," Schmutzer said.

"So you had to break Woody out before the hearing," Reynolds said. "You know I made you before you left the courtroom the other day."

"I know," Schmutzer said. "When you are raised by an uncle who was a Nazi war criminal, who smuggled himself into this country and lived under an assumed identity for sixty years, you learn how to tell when someone is getting too close to the truth. He taught me how to fly under the radar and when to cut and run."

Reynolds was winding down. "So you drop the old photo of Waylon and Woody on Maggie's doorstep and wait for us to find the escapees." Shot Glass thought for a minute. He sorted all the pieces of the file in his mind as he searched for things that didn't fit.

"How did you come up with that picture anyway? I thought there were only two copies, one for Woody, the other that he sent to the captain of the boat who took it," Reynolds said.

"You probably need to examine it a little more closely," Schmutzer said.

Shot Glass knew the picture by heart. He played it in his head, zoomed in on the details. Then it came to him.

"The captain of that other boat was your uncle?" he said.

"You were the young boy with him?"

Schmutzer shrugged.

Shot Glass went back to his theory of the case. "So you anticipated that I wouldn't arrest the jail breakers on the spot and that you could lure me on the boat with your proposition for an alternative course of action."

"Sounds plausible," Linus said.

"So that means your plan has worked like a charm so far. All the pieces are in place," Reynolds said. "What happens next?"

Schmutzer looked at his wrist watch.

"If everything fits together just right, you will have the answer to that question in about three hours and forty minutes," Schmutzer said.

Reynolds looked at his watch. He made the calculation.

"Six fifteen," Reynolds said.

Linus nodded.

Chapter 38

THEOPHILUS FRANCIS FOUND a bucket with soapy water and a scrub brush inside the cabin door and began to busy himself. He scrubbed the deck, wiped mildew off the seats, checked the various compartments for trash. After an hour or so, he dropped the brush in the bucket and walked to the stern where Odd Sheffield held a long fiberglass fishing pole with an open face reel.

Sheffield had the end of a thirty pound test line in one hand, a cigar-shaped lure in the other. He had already threaded the line from the reel through the loops along the length of the pole. The balsa wood lure, green with orange spots to simulate gills, was about five inches long. It had a treble hook on the business end. Francis watched as Odd fed the end of the line twice through the lure's eye, then weaved the free end of the line ten times around the strand of wire connected to the reel. As the last step, Sheffield slipped the wire's end between the small insertion point he had left next to the lure's eye, grabbed the tag end with his teeth, pulled it tight until it snugged up against the faux bait fish. He took his right thumb and index finger and worked the knot until he got it just the way he wanted it. He held his work up in the sunlight and admired it. He grinned.

"Ain't no grouper going to break that sumbitch," he said to Francis.

"I reckon not," Theo said.

Sheffield put the rod and reel down and picked up a smaller one. He started to thread the line through the rod loops when Theo stopped him.

"I've been thinking about what you said about us last night," he said.

Sheffield wrinkled his brow.

"What's that?"

"You know. That deal about how we've always been fuck ups and always will be."

"Yeah. What about it?" Odd said.

"I don't want my life to go down like that. I'm not ready to give up hope yet," Francis said.

Odd put down the fishing gear and swiveled around in his chair to face Francis.

"I don't want mine to go that way either, Francis. I'm sorry I said that to you. I didn't mean it. But you know we're in deep shit when we get off this boat."

"I know," Francis said.

"Unless..." Odd said.

"Unless what?

"Unless we can show what we're made of out here. You know the doc didn't break us out to take us fishing. Something's about to come down," Sheffield said.

"I know. And it ain't going to be pretty," Theo said.

"Some folks may get killed; some may get saved. We need to be sure we're on the right side," Sheffield said.

"You mean the winning side?"

"I mean the right side," Sheffield said.

"I've spent most of my life on the wrong side," Theo said. "I beat the shit out of guys who didn't have it coming, put my momma in the hospital with a heart attack from worrying about me. But today when the killing starts, I plan to be righteous."

Francis shook Sheffield's hand. "You can count on me, Odd. I think it's time we got a fresh start. Maybe we'll be partners when it's all said and done."

"I'd like that, Francis. I surely would."

Chapter 39

SHOT GLASS SAW the massive chunks of granite ahead that comprised the jetties, the man-made buttresses to the pass where St. Andrew Bay opened into the Gulf of Mexico. He could see a few people on the beach at the state park to his west, Shell Island to his east. It was an ebb tide and the dark water of the bay flooded into the pale shallow waters of the ocean.

He checked his watch.

It was five o'clock.

He looked over at Schmutzer. As if on cue, Schmutzer got up and walked to him.

"Detective Reynolds, I think the time has come for me to be forthcoming," Linus said.

"I wondered when that was going to happen," Reynolds said

Linus sloughed off the remark. "You are here because I need your fire power. We all do. I can handle a gun, but not like you. We will have to make split-second decisions. All that I've learned about you says that it is in such a situation when you are at your best," Linus said.

"I'm flattered," Reynolds said. "Now cut the bullshit."

Linus continued. "I can tell you this much. I expect us to draw fire from two sides. We will have to keep moving or they will cut us to pieces. The enemy will have superior weapons; we will have the element of surprise," Schmutzer said.

"Who will drive the boat?" Reynolds asked.

"This is Captain's Woody's mission. I have complete confidence that he will rise to the occasion. He will lead us to victory or he will die trying," Linus said.

Reynolds looked through the cabin door at Woody.

"No doubt about it. But before I lay my life down for you, I want to know why you're in this deal. What gives between you and Woody Wilson?"

Linus looked out at the ocean, took note of the positions of a few pleasure boats, glanced at his watch.

"Fair enough," he said. "When the Allies liberated the concentration camp, my dad was at death's door. Woody was one of the GIs who gave blood to save him. During dad's recuperation, Woody visited him often at the hospital and they became friends, blood brothers if you wish. When they parted ways, my dad, Horatio, pledged to Woody that the Schmutzer family would never forget his kindness."

"What about your uncle?" Reynolds asked.

"He fled the camp well ahead of its liberation and entered the underground network that sheltered and aided Nazis who were on the run. Ultimately he arrived in this country and showed up at our home place in Franklin, Tennessee. Horatio, as only he could do, welcomed him back into the family fold despite the cruel treatment he had received at his hands. I think he did so because he knew his time was short," Linus said.

"Was he sick?" Reynolds asked.

"He was sick at heart. Coupled with the deprivations of the camp, it proved too much for him. My mother's death in childbirth was the *coup de grace*. He took his own life but not before he made a deal with the devil."

"The devil was in the form of Linus Schmutzer, your uncle?" Shot Glass said.

"He was. Horatio agreed to kill himself so that his brother might step into his shoes," Linus said without emotion.

Reynolds shook his head as if he heard Linus' words but couldn't find a place to put them.

"And what did he get in return for this pact?" Reynolds asked.

"Linus made two promises to him. First that he would raise me as his son and sole heir; second that he and I would watch over and protect Woody so long as he lived."

"So in order to protect him, you kidnapped him, took him away from Maggie and almost killed him? Then you were prepared to testify against him in Court to ensure that he would spend the rest of his life in prison?" Shot Glass said.

"I did all those things," Schmutzer said.

"It doesn't sound like you were holding up your end of the bargain, Linus," Shot Glass said.

"That's where you are wrong, Shot Glass," Linus said. "You know better than most people that things are seldom as they appear. I don't have time to explain everything now. Perhaps after we face the challenge at hand, we can talk again."

"And what if we don't have another chance to chit chat?"

Linus reached into his pocket and removed an object. He handed it to Reynolds. "In that case, take this to Ocean Bank in Seagrove Beach. The bank president already has his instructions."

Shot Glass studied the item in his hand, a pendant key ring on which hung an old brass key. The pendant was formed into the shape of the letters *HS*.

"*HS* stands for Horatio Schmutzer, I assume."

"My father, may God rest his soul," Schmutzer said. "You might want to put it somewhere safe." He moved away from Reynolds and sat down on the bench on the starboard side of the boat. He looked east towards the horizon.

Shot Glass slipped the keepsake in his pants pocket and patted the spot with his hand.

Linus held up his left wrist and tapped his watch with his right index finger.

"It won't be long now. It's time to arm ourselves," he said.

Chapter 40

SHOT GLASS WAVED at Waylon. When he saw Reynolds' signal, Waylon got up from the bow and made his way toward Shot Glass, bent over with one hand on the bow rail and the other secured on a steel grab bar on the side of the cabin.

"Take a position next to your dad inside, and stay there until this thing goes down," Reynolds told him. "And put this in your pocket. If they board us it might come in handy." He stuck the snub-nosed .38-caliber revolver in Waylon's hand.

"*They* who?" he asked.

"*They* I don't know yet," Reynolds said.

Waylon saw that Reynolds was wearing his shoulder holster. The butt of his Smith and Wesson protruded out of the front of his windbreaker.

Waylon handled the gun like it was a cracked vial of HIV virus but stuck it in his front pants pocket and walked through the cabin door, sat down in the chair next to Woody.

Reynolds followed him into the cabin.

"Captain Woody, we've heard reports recently of a bunch of hooligans who are roaming these waters. I thought you might want this just in case someone suspicious approached us," he said.

He handed Woody the Kimber Model 1911 .45-caliber semi-automatic.

Woody balanced the gun in his hand, racked the slide to feed a round in the chamber. With the hammer in firing position, he engaged the safety and laid the pistol on the dash in front of him.

"Thanks, son. They'd better steer clear of the *Miss Maggie* if they know what's good for 'em," Woody said.

"You got that right, Captain Woody," Reynolds said. He glanced at Waylon before he turned and walked out of the cabin.

On deck, Schmutzer took the padlock off the foot locker and threw open the lid. He got out his AK 47 and propped it next to him. Then he pulled out two more AKs and two loaded magazines. He walked across the deck to Odd Sheffield and held up one of the rifles.

"You know how to use this, don't you, Sheffield?" Schmutzer said.

"You know I do, Doc," Sheffield said.

"In a few minutes, you'll recognize who the targets are. I suggest you kill them before they kill us."

"That was the plan I followed in 'Nam. It worked out all right," Sheffield said.

Schmutzer looked at Theo who stood next to Odd.

"Theo, can you shoot?" Linus said.

"I was killing 'gators in the bayous with AKs before I could walk," Theo said.

"Unlike 'gators, the guys we are about to meet will be shooting back. Can you handle it?" Schmutzer said.

"They'll know they have been in a fight, doc," Francis said.

"You heard what I told Sheffield. You have the same orders. Don't stop shooting 'til you know they are all dead."

"I understand," Francis said. His eyes were as clear as a dry gin martini, his cheeks pink with anticipation.

"Good," Schmutzer said. He handed Theo the assault weapon, went back to his usual spot and sat down with his rifle across his lap.

Reynolds sat down next to Schmutzer again.

"I don't want to mess with your plan, Linus, but it strikes me that if we want to maintain the element of surprise in whatever is about to happen, we might want to at least pretend like we are doing something besides laying in wait for somebody," Shot Glass said.

Schmutzer thought about it. Before he could answer, Woody cut the engines and the boat settled down in the water, drifted parallel to the beach three hundred yards off shore.

Woody yelled out the cabin door. "Doc Smooth, this contraption says we have arrived." He pointed at the GPS. "Break out the fishing gear. Time's a wasting. It'll be dark soon."

"Imagine that," Schmutzer said as he looked at Shot Glass.

"I should have known," Reynolds said as he returned Linus' look. He walked to the stern of the boat where Sheffield handed him the rig with the cigar-shaped lure.

Reynolds cast the artificial bait into the salt water and worked it back towards the boat. Theo grabbed the smaller spinning rig and cast his lure off the port side towards the beach.

"I bet I catch one before you do, Detective Reynolds," he said.

"In your dreams, Francis," Reynolds said. He drew his pole back and sailed the bait towards a dark spot where he figured the big fish were hiding in the weeds. As he reeled the line in, he glanced at his watch.

It was five minutes after six.

Chapter 41

MAGGIE WAITED BY the phone for three hours after Waylon left the condo with Shot Glass to go to the house in Point Washington. When she received no word from her son, she took to the road.

She drove to the Methodist church near the public boat ramp, got out her map and oriented herself. She found the road she needed and eased along until she found Reynolds' deserted unmarked police cruiser on the side of the lane. She parked next to it, got out and worked her way along the tree line until she acquired a good view of the structure that stood at the address on the old photo.

It was a new house, one that she hadn't seen before. But something about the location seemed familiar to her as if she had been there in a former life. She looked at the homes up and down the lane, all about the same age, but nothing jogged her memory.

"It's been too long, I guess," she said.

She remained hidden in the thick underbrush as she watched and waited for half an hour. Finally, she crept out of her cover and approached the cottage.

She circled the dwelling and peered through the shuttered windows. The rooms were dark. Nothing moved inside. In the back yard she saw the board walk that led to a covered boat slip on the edge of the marsh. She saw no boat docked at the slip.

"Where are you, Woody?" she said to herself as she walked along the planks that hovered above the swamp. When she got to the boat house, she looked up and down the creek and saw no vessels on the water.

For the first time she saw Woody's old green skiff tied to the pier.

"How in God's name did that get here?" she said.

She walked to the edge of the pier above the place where the row boat lay in the water and looked at it, a priceless treasure now abandoned, empty and lifeless.

Someone had built a ladder down to the water by nailing random boards a foot or so apart to one of the pilings that supported the pier. The skiff bobbed next to the bottom rung.

Maggie put her purse handle around her neck so that the purse hung against her back, turned her back to the water, got down on her hands and knees and lowered herself a step at a time down the ladder. When she got next to the jon boat, she reached out with her left foot and pulled it close to the pier. She held on to the next to bottom board with both hands and placed her feet as near the middle of the boat as she could reach. She used her weight to wedge the jon boat against the piling and let go with her hands. She staggered for a minute while the boat shifted under her feet, steadied herself and sat down on the cross timber that served as the skiff's rowing platform.

She was out of breath and nauseated from exertion. A rope tied to the pier floated next to the boat. She reached into the water with one hand, grabbed it and pulled the flat bow of the boat into the shade of the wooden deck floor above her. A green turtle stuck its snout out of the water, took a breath and left her alone while she rested.

After ten minutes, Maggie felt strong enough to proceed with her mission. She picked up the oars, one in each hand, and began to ply them through the murky water of the slough. She backed the skiff into the creek and turned the bow to the middle of the channel. Then she rowed up the creek to a sharp turn where it meandered along the backside of waterfront homes. She saw no sign of any other boats except those that hung on slings under boat house canopies.

When she came to the end of the line of houses, she threw her weight against the oars and rotated the skiff one hundred and eighty degrees, paddled her way back to her original point of departure.

She passed the boat house where she had boarded the skiff and continued on the creek until she reached the junction where it opened onto a wider expanse of water, the backwater of the bay. She rowed a couple of hundred yards farther before she became too tired to continue. She pulled the oars out of the water, laid them in the center of the boat, put her hands on her knees and took a deep breath. She looked from side to side, in front and behind her. She listened for the familiar whine of an outboard engine but heard only birds squawking in the reeds and the hum of flying insects.

"Woody," she yelled. "Where are you, Woody?"

Her plea echoed off the still water and returned to her unrequited.

She had left her straw bonnet at the condo, and the late October sun beat down on her face. For a moment she thought she might faint. She placed her arms behind her with her hands against the wooden deck of the skiff, braced herself, leaned back and closed her eyes.

Soon her exhaustion turned to drowsiness. She lay down on her side in the small craft and fell asleep. As day turned to evening, the old green skiff, the jon boat hand-made by Woody Wilson seventy years before, carried her on the tributary's slow relentless current towards the broad waters of Choctawhatchee Bay.

Chapter 42

ON HIS FOURTH cast towards the dark spot off the stern, Shot Glass felt a tug on his line. "I've got a bite," he said to Odd who stood next to him watching.

"If it's a grouper, he will play with the bait a minute before he takes it. Don't set the hook yet," Sheffield said.

Reynolds waited a ten count before he felt a stronger weight on the end of the line. Odd saw the line grow taut.

"Now," Sheffield said.

Shot Glass jerked the pole towards the boat with all his strength.

Theo yelled at Woody.

"Captain Woody, he's got one. Gun it."

Woody had turned to watch the fisherman. On Francis' signal, he pushed the throttle all the way forward, and the boat lurched ahead in the water. The men on the deck shifted their weight to maintain their balance while Reynolds wrestled with the fish.

Francis held up his right hand with his palm toward Woody, then clinched his fist and pumped it in the air.

When Woody saw Francis' gesture, he pulled the throttle back all the way, and the boat settled in the water.

"Keep the line tight, Detective Reynolds," Theo said. "He'll try to run to cover."

Reynolds nodded at Theo. He cranked the pole over his head and then lowered it toward the water as he worked the handle of the reel to take up the slack in the line.

Theo grabbed a three foot gaff from a storage bin near the stern. The steel hook on the end of the gaff hungered to find its home in the mouth of the underwater monster.

Reynolds made headway with his prey. He moved to the starboard side of the boat, placed his right foot on the gunwale, pulled and cranked.

"Don't let him run under the boat, Shot Glass," Sheffield said.

While Reynolds fought with the fish, Francis and Sheffield cheered him on. Schmutzer entered the cabin. He reached into a cabinet near the pilot's station and took out a spotlight with a six foot cord curled around it.

He exited the cabin and made his way to the bow where he mounted the spotlight on a metal receiver. He unwound the cord and stuck the end of it into a twelve volt outlet. He flicked a switch on the light to ensure that it worked, rotated it 270 degrees, turned it off and let it hang angled towards the front of the bow.

When he finished with the light, Schmutzer returned to his seat, picked up his AK and moved across the deck to the port side. He sat down, placed the butt of the rifle on the deck and put his right hand on the rifle barrel about a foot below the muzzle. He looked to the west and scanned the shoreline.

"I think he's about to break the surface," Shot Glass yelled.

Theo moved next to Reynolds and leaned forward to watch the water, the gaff in his left hand, his right hand on the steel rail of the gunwale.

"Give me a shot at him," Francis said to Reynolds.

Reynolds pumped the pole again, first up in the air, then down near the water's surface. He yanked the pole hard in the air, and Francis saw an object a couple of feet under the water. It looked to be about three feet long, gray and splotched with brown markings like a clown's outfit from a third-rate circus.

"It's a gag grouper. A big one. Keep after him, Detective Reynolds," he said. "It doesn't count unless you can land him."

"Hide and watch, Theo," Reynolds said. He was breathing hard and sweat ran down his face. He put his back into it and groaned as he tried to raise the grouper to the surface.

For a second, the fish broke the surface, and Theo leaned his body against the gunwale. He reached the gaff towards the fish, but the fish dove out of his reach and hovered below the surface, still fighting the hook.

"He's almost done. Let him tire himself out a minute, then try it again," Sheffield said to Reynolds.

Reynolds kept the line tight as he leaned back and rested for a second.

"If the sumbitch doesn't give up pretty quick, he may drag me in the water with him," Reynolds said. He wished he hadn't cancelled his membership at the gym.

Schmutzer checked his watch. At exactly six-fifteen he caught his first glimpse of an ocean-going vessel as it moved from the west to the east in the shipping channel. Soon the contours of a double-hulled oil tanker appeared in the dim light of dusk. The giant ship sat low in the water from its heavy cargo. It moved across the surface of the sea like a rhinoceros on the prowl with its head lowered, prepared to charge anyone that dared enter its domain. With its running lights on, the tanker looked like a small continent separated from the mainland, adrift, a self-contained universe that held no allegiance to any sovereign except oil.

While Reynolds prepared for his last thrust against the grouper and Theo and Odd watched the fish just below the surface, Schmutzer focused his attention on a narrow inlet two hundred yards west of their position. He saw two boats emerge, one behind the other.

The first boat was a thirty-one foot Contender with a dark blue hull, the second a twenty-seven foot white Cape Horn. The center console boats sported twin 350 Yamaha outboards. Their T-tops had navy coverings.

Each boat had a crew of three. The men were dressed in black neoprene wet suits, with black diving hoods on their heads, black diving masks on their faces and black snorkels dangling next to their mouths.

The boats bumped over the waves near shore, and the crew members looked toward the boat to their east. When they saw Reynolds fighting the fish, they turned away and checked the tanker's position.

When they cleared the breaking waves, the captains gunned the engines, and the two boats blasted through the water on a collision course with the tanker.

When Schmutzer saw the crews turn their attention away from the *Nothing Left to Lose*, he got up and walked next to Shot Glass.

Reynolds was straining against the fish. "I can almost reach him. Pull, Reynolds. Pull," Theo said.

Schmutzer took a large pocket knife out of his pocket, flipped the blade open with a jerk of his wrist, grabbed the line that ran from Reynolds' pole to the grouper and cut it with one stroke.

Reynolds fell backwards and Odd caught him before he hit the deck.

"What the fuck?" Francis said as he watched the grouper descend out of sight in the water.

"It's time," Schmutzer said. "The next five minutes will tell whether we live or die." He closed his knife, stuck it in his pocket, walked to his rifle and took it in both hands while Reynolds, Sheffield and Francis stared at him.

"Dear Mother of God," Francis said. He pointed at the tanker and the two boats that raced towards it. He threw the gaff on the deck, picked up an AK and tossed it to Odd. He grabbed the other one, kneeled on the deck and sighted in the Contender.

Schmutzer placed his hand on the barrel of Francis' rifle, pressed it down toward the deck.

"Not yet, Theo," he said. "We have to make every shot count."

Schmutzer yelled toward the cabin.

"Captain Woody, the battle is joined. Put us on top of those pirates."

"You got it, Doc Smooth. Praise the Lord and pass the ammunition," Woody yelled back at him.

Woody pushed the throttle full forward and the *Nothing Left to Lose* leaped up on the water's surface. He cut the wheel hard starboard and set his course for the mid-point between the sterns of the Contender and the Cape Horn. He cranked the window in front of him open to the salt air, took the Kimber in his left hand and steered with his right.

In the seat next to him Waylon watched Woody.

The old warrior had come back to life.

Chapter 43

WITH WOODY IN hot pursuit of the pirates, Reynolds and Schmutzer moved forward and held to the steel grab bars on the side of the cabin as they watched the boats in front of them.

Reynolds leaned over to Schmutzer.

"How in the hell did you orchestrate this?" he said.

"I didn't. I just knew it was coming down and thought it might present an opportunity for some people to rehabilitate themselves," Schmutzer said.

"And how was it that you knew a terrorist attack on an oil tanker was coming down?" Reynolds asked.

The Parker bounced hard on the three foot chop as Woody closed on the pirates.

Schmutzer replied. "My uncle left Germany a rich man, rich from the booty he extracted from the prisoners in the camps. He lived underground the rest of his life, but he managed his money well. He forged alliances with people like him, people who operated outside the law, and converted his small fortune into a large one. In his later years, I became his ambassador. When you have those sorts of connections, you hear things," Schmutzer said. It was a matter-of-fact statement, nothing more.

"You mean CIA-type connections?" Shot Glass said.

"CIA, Mafia, Al-Qaida, they're all pretty much the same. Sometimes you are on the same team; sometimes you are trying to kill each other. It all depends on the project *du jour*," Schmutzer said. His delivery was casual, ice water in his veins.

Reynolds thought about it.

He had changed teams a few times himself. "I take it these guys aren't your usual pirates. They plan to blow up the tanker," he said.

"Unless we stop them," Schmutzer said.

"So whatever we do to them is in self-defense and as patriots who seek to preserve our country's freedom?" Reynolds said.

"I suspect that is the way the citizens of the United States and any law enforcement personnel would see it," Schmutzer said.

"Me, too," Reynolds said. "Let's give 'em hell, Doc."

"I'll take the captain of the boat on the left. You take the captain on the right," Schmutzer said.

"Give me the sign when you're ready to fire," Shot Glass said.

The two men separated and moved onto the bow of the ship, Schmutzer on the port side, Reynolds on the starboard. The two boats ahead of them ran with their lights off. In the half light, they became vague objects shrouded in salt spray, not the defined targets a sharp shooter needed. Shot Glass drew his .357, laid out flat on the deck and braced the elbow of his right arm for the shot. Schmutzer leaned against the forward wall of the cabin and took dead aim with his rifle.

Woody came at the terrorists' boats as if he would ram them. When he closed to within fifteen yards of the rear of the boats, he sounded his horn and the captains looked behind them as they realized for the first time that they were under attack. They swung their pilot wheels in opposite directions to create some distance between them and Woody, but it was too late.

Schmutzer yelled, "Now!"

"It's a lot easier shot with an AK than with a pistol," Shot Glass said under his breath.

Shot Glass fired two rounds, and the captain of the Contender collapsed to his knees, and then fell face first on the deck. At the same time, Reynolds heard three explosions from the AK to his left. He saw the captain of the Cape Horn as he fell forward on the wheel.

The tanker trudged through the water a hundred yards ahead of the pirates. There was no activity on deck.

The pilotless boats continued to plow through the water in the broad arcs created by their deceased captains' actions. When the surviving crew members realized they were under fire, one man in each boat stepped to the wheel and took control of their vessels while the others opened fire on the *Nothing Left To Lose* with micro Uzis.

As the 9mm bullets showered down on his ship, Captain Woody yanked the wheel hard left. As the boat changed course, Theo got an open shot and emptied his magazine into one of the gunmen.

The impact of the shots spun the man around. He staggered against the gunwale, tried to catch himself on the railing and then flipped over the side of the Contender. As his boat moved away from him, his body bobbed face down in the sea.

The captain of the Cape Horn cut his engines and Woody blew past him no more than ten yards off his port side. When Woody's boat came next to the pirate ship, the gunman opened up on Theo. He took a round in his left shoulder and fell backwards on the deck.

Odd Sheffield threw himself on top of Theo as the bullets riddled the hull of the boat.

"Stay down, Theo," Sheffield said.

"I'm hit," Francis said. "But I think it's a clean wound." He held his right hand against the bullet hole and applied pressure to it to stop the bleeding.

Woody threw the boat in a tight circle until he came around on a collision course with the Cape Horn. Odd dragged Theo across the deck to the relative cover of the rear wall of the cabin. He retrieved his AK, crouched down and threw the rifle against his shoulder.

"Give me a shot, Captain Woody," he yelled.

"You'll have one in just a second, Odd. Wait 'til I turn her hard right," Woody said.

"Aye, Aye, Captain," Sheffield said. He put his finger on the trigger of the assault weapon.

Schmutzer crawled to the spotlight and lay face down on the forward deck as Woody pursued his target.

Shot Glass ran to the stern, picked up Theo's AK, jammed a new magazine in it and knelt down as he waited for the Contender to make its run at them.

Just before he would have rammed the Cape Horn, Woody cranked the wheel hard right. When he did, Sheffield opened up on the gunman. His one shot struck the man in the head and he collapsed on the deck.

"It don't take no full magazine of shooting to get the job done," Sheffield said. He looked down at Theo who tried to smile.

The lone pilot that remained on the Cape Horn pulled his ship hard right, too, to bring himself next to Woody. He grabbed for his Uzi. The second before the ships side-swiped each other, Schmutzer turned on the spotlight and shined it in the captain's eyes. The captain, blinded for an instant, held up his hand to block the bright beam of light.

Schmutzer leaped to his feet, ran across the bow and hurled himself in the direction of the pirate ship. He landed on both feet, rolled once on the deck and came up with his knife opened in his right hand.

The pirate captain twisted his body towards Schmutzer with his Uzi in his hand. Schmutzer, like a major league pitcher giving it all he had with his best fastball, threw his knife at the captain. It lodged in his neck and the captain grabbed his throat as he pulled the trigger on the Uzi. The burst of stray bullets struck Schmutzer in the leg, the torso and the left arm. He tried to remain on his feet, but crashed down on his knees, fell forward on the deck. The captain fell next to him, dead.

"Holy shit," Shot Glass said as he watched Schmutzer in hand to hand combat on the Cape Horn. Then he heard the big engines of the Contender and looked behind him.

The Contender's captain saw he was alone. He broke off his pursuit of the *Nothing Left to Lose* and set a course that would bring him alongside the tanker. As he ran flat out towards the huge ship, he reached in a cargo box and drew out another weapon, a rocket launcher.

"You've got to get me closer to him, Captain Woody," Shot Glass shouted. "He's about to blow the tanker."

Woody gave the boat all he had as he caromed across the waves towards the terrorist's ship.

"Take the wheel, son," he said to Waylon. "Keep her running straight at him."

Waylon stood behind the wheel and piloted the boat.

Woody grabbed the Kimber in his left hand, stuck it through the open window and fired. The Contender captain heard the shots, looked back at the Parker boat and realized he was out of Woody's range. He put the rocket launcher on his shoulder and sited in the tanker.

Shot Glass ran to the bow, threw himself flat on the deck and raised the AK. He felt the tremor in his hands, braced his arms against the deck to quell it.

"God, if you're out there listening, give me just this one last shot and I'll leave you alone from now on," Reynolds said.

The pirate captain put his finger on the trigger of the rocket launcher.

Reynolds squeezed off one round.

Chapter 44

WAYLON PULLED THE boat up next to the Contender. Woody stood at the bow with Shot Glass who held his Smith and Wesson .357 in his right hand. Sheffield shined the spotlight on the deck of the Contender.

"Looks like you got him," Woody said.

"Right through the heart," Reynolds said.

The men saw the terrorists on the deck. The man with the rocket launcher had fallen on top of the boat's captain. The rocket launcher lay next to his hand with its payload still intact.

"That was a hell of a shot," Woody said. He stumbled as he stood on the bow, almost lost his balance. "I'm not feeling too good all of a sudden."

Shot Glass looked at Woody and saw a blood stain that had spread across the front of his shirt. "Let's take a look at you, Captain Woody," Reynolds said. He helped Woody to the open deck behind the cabin, sat him down on a bench.

When he unbuttoned Woody's shirt, he saw the entry wound of a bullet.

"Looks like a 9mm," Odd said. "It must have come from one of those Uzis."

Reynolds had Woody lie down on the bench. He fetched the ship's first aid kit, poured some alcohol on the wound and wiped off as much blood as he could with cotton gauze. Woody had his eyes closed. He turned his head.

"Red, right, return," he whispered.

The men looked at each other and didn't know what to make of Woody's words.

"That's his way of telling us to get him home safely," Waylon said. "Do you think he's going to be all right, Shot Glass?"

"We have to get him to the hospital as soon as we can. I don't see an exit wound, so I suspect the bullet is still in there. He may have some internal bleeding," Reynolds said.

Waylon went in the cabin and picked up the radio to call in a mayday. Before he could make the call, he saw a bright light.

"United States Coast Guard. Prepare to be boarded," the voice on the bull horn said. Two aluminum-hulled Coast Guard vessels pulled up alongside them. Soldiers stood on the deck with their rifles pointed at the crew of the *Nothing Left To Lose*.

Reynolds flashed his badge. "Sherwood Reynolds, special investigator, Nashville PD," he shouted at the Coast Guard contingency. "We have two wounded on board that need immediate medical attention."

The skipper of one of the Coast Guard vessels came to the railing. "We received a distress call from the tanker. They said there was a war going on out here. It looks like the bad guys came out on the losing end of the battle," he said.

"There are four more bodies around here somewhere," Reynolds said. "The guys on that tanker don't know how lucky they are that we came along when we did."

"Oh yes they do, Detective Reynolds. I can assure you of that," the skipper said.

Members of the Coast Guard boarded the ship, placed Woody and Theo on stretchers and transferred them to one of the Coast Guard vessels. Waylon got on the boat with Woody.

"We'll get them to the hospital right now," the skipper said. "Can you guys make it back to shore in that boat?"

"She's brought us this far, captain. I think she can get us home," Reynolds said.

"I'll bet she can, too," the skipper said. He knew a good boat when he saw one. "Report to the Coast Guard station in Panama City. We'll have someone waiting to bring you to the hospital." The captain saluted the men and the Coast Guard vessel that carried Woody, Theo and Waylon roared off to the east, its emergency lights illuminating the black water.

The other Coast Guard vessel circled the Contender with the two dead men in it.

"I guess we're free to go," Shot Glass said to Odd Sheffield. "Do you know how to drive a boat?"

"Does a wild bear shit in the woods?" Sheffield said.

"Well then why don't you get us on out of here while the getting is good?"

When the *Nothing Left To Lose* was several hundred yards from the remaining Coast Guard ship, Shot Glass spoke to Odd. "We need to see if we can find the boat with Schmutzer on it. I didn't see any reason to make a big deal about it with them." He motioned with his head towards the Coast Guard vessel.

Sheffield nodded. "I think I can retrace our course pretty well. Maybe we'll get lucky and spot the Cape Horn."

They worked their way across the water. Reynolds turned on the spotlight and panned it from side to side in front of the ship. The men saw nothing that resembled a boat.

When they were fifty yards off the beach, the spotlight fell on the cove where the pirates had laid in wait before they commenced the attack on the tanker.

"Can you get her in there?" Reynolds asked Odd.

"Yeah, it's high tide. It shouldn't be a problem," Sheffield said.

He eased the ship into the cove. When they rounded a slight bend, they saw the Cape Horn, run ashore, stuck on a sand bar. Reynolds threw the light on the boat.

"Ahoy there," he cried out. "Is there anyone aboard?"

There was no answer.

"Get as close as you can without running aground," Reynolds said.

Sheffield idled into the shallow water. A few yards from shore he stopped. "That's about it," he said.

Shot Glass took off his shoes, tucked a flashlight in his belt and let himself down into the water off the swim platform on the transom. He breast stroked to shore with his head above water, climbed up on the bow of the boat from the beach side.

Odd saw Reynolds shine the flashlight on the deck of the boat, bend down for a minute, walk to the bow again and hop down on the beach. He swam back to the boat, climbed the ladder and sat down.

"So?" Sheffield asked.

"There is one body on board, a pirate with a knife stuck in his neck. I can't be for sure, but I may have seen some foot prints and a blood trail that led across the dunes," Reynolds said.

Odd looked at Reynolds. "You can't bullshit me, Shot Glass. You know what you saw. You're not going after him?"

"No, I think it's better if we just leave it alone. Don't you?"

"Works for me," Odd said.

He took the boat out of the cove into the Gulf, moved slowly through the breaking waves. When he reached calm water he pushed the throttle all the way forward as he set his course for Panama City.

"This run is for Captain Woody," Odd said to Reynolds. The wind blew strong across their faces. The spray doused them through the open captain's window. Sheffield poked Shot Glass in the arm and pointed south. There they saw the lights of an enormous ship, an oil tanker that moved undisturbed through the safe waters of the Gulf of Mexico.

Chapter 45

WHEN MAGGIE WOKE up, night had fallen. For a minute, she was disoriented. She started to stand and felt the jon boat lilt to one side before she realized she was on the water. She sat back down and steadied the skiff.

She looked around and saw lights in the houses along the shore, hundreds of yards north and south of her. She realized she was adrift in the middle of Choctawhatchee Bay. For a second she panicked, but then she gathered herself.

"Woody will have a cow if he ever learns about this," she said to herself.

She decided to call 911.

They will have someone out here to pick me up in an hour or so," she said to calm herself.

She fumbled in her purse and took out her cell phone. It was an old flip phone and when she tried to open it in the dark, she bobbled it in her hands. When she thought she had it, it slipped away from her, hit the gunwale of the skiff and fell overboard into the salt water. "What an old fool I have become," she said as she leaned to look over the side of the boat into the thirty foot deep water.

She told herself to formulate Plan B. She knew if she rowed north or south, she would have to make landfall. So she took up the oars and dug into the water with them. In the moonless night, she could see nothing in the water, not even the water itself. She felt like she made no headway with the oars, like a person on a treadmill who runs for an hour and finds himself in the same place as he began. She kept at it for thirty minutes before she lifted the oars out of the black liquid of the bay and rested. The lights of the south shore were no closer than when she first started rowing.

To the west she could make out a trail of lights that crossed the bay in a high arc.

"That has to be the Highway 331 Bridge," she thought. She knew from many trips under that bridge with Woody on the *Miss Maggie* that the road there jutted out in the bay before the span of the bridge began. She calculated that her shortest journey to land was west and south towards the point where the bridge and the road bed met.

She was beyond exhausted, but she grabbed the oars and pulled them against the water. She rowed ten minutes, rested ten, rowed ten, rested ten. After two hours she was able to make out a black solidness, the boulders that lined the side of the road bed.

She pulled harder with strength she thought had vanished. After fifteen minutes, she felt a thump as the bow of the boat struck something. She turned to look off the bow, crawled on her hands and knees to the front of the skiff. She had jammed the jon boat between two of the boulders. The stern, still afloat, rose and fell as it pulsed in tune with the energy of the great body of water that had been her home for almost twelve hours.

Maggie considered staying in the boat 'til morning when she was sure a passing motorist would find her. But she feared the boat might break free in the night and strand her on the bay again.

She took off her shoes and threw them as far as she could towards land, then turned with her back to the boulders and lowered her feet into the water until she felt solid rock. Her foot slipped on the slick, hard surface and she held on to the side of the jon boat as she searched for sure footing. She found a flat spot and rested her weight on one leg as she tried to make out the contours of the jetty.

When she thought she was ready, she pushed away from the boat with both hands, twisted her body and fell on a boulder to her left. She hugged the rock with both arms until she got her feet under her. She wedged her right foot in a crack formed at the junction of her rock and one next to it and climbed a little higher out of the water. With half an hour of work, she made it to the last row of boulders between her and the grass on the shoulder of the road.

"Even this old girl can jump that far," she said.

She put both her feet together, counted to three and stepped out into the air in front of her. When she pushed off, she slipped and fell short of the grass three feet in front of her. She tumbled into the water and slid down the side of the bank. She grabbed a sharp rock on the shore with her hands. She fought to find her footing but her strength was gone.

She clung to the rock and prayed for daylight.

Chapter 46

IT WAS EIGHT-THIRTY by the time Sheffield and Reynolds arrived at the Coast Guard station in Panama City. Guardsmen escorted them ashore, put them in a military Humvee and drove them to Gulf Coast Medical Center.

At the front desk the receptionist directed them to surgical ICU. When they walked in the intensive care unit waiting area, they saw Thag Clemons asleep in the corner. He had his feet propped up in the chair next to him, an open law book balanced on his ample stomach. There was a Kentucky Fried Chicken Styrofoam cup filled with Camel cigarette butts on the coffee table next to him, a No Smoking sign pasted on the wall three feet above his head.

Thag's snoring dominated the room. Family members of other patients had left the waiting area and camped out in the hall. Shot Glass walked over to Thag and looked at him a minute. The other family members watched and hoped he would arrest him on the spot.

"Counselor?" Reynolds said.

Thag snorted one more time and then opened his eyes.

"Shot Glass Reynolds, you're a sight for sore eyes, man," Thag said. He pushed himself out of the chair, shook Reynolds' hand and placed his left hand on his shoulder. He started to hug him but thought better of it.

"Pythagoras Clemons, I would like to introduce my good friend, Odessa Sheffield," Shot Glass said as he motioned toward Odd.

Thag extended his hand to Sheffield. "I've heard a lot about you from Woody Wilson, Mr. Sheffield. You've been a godsend for him."

Sheffield's face lit up. He threw his shoulders back and lifted his chin when he replied.

"Mr. Woody told me at least a hundred times how much he liked having a lawyer named Thag, Mr. Clemons. It's a great pleasure to meet you." He sounded like a foreign ambassador making his opening remarks at an official state dinner at the White House.

"How's Woody, Thag?" Reynolds asked.

"He was in surgery for an hour and half. A few minutes ago the doctor came through here and told me he was stable. They removed a 9mm slug that lodged in his ribcage. Best they can tell they have stopped the bleeding They have him doped up and don't expect him to wake up for another six hours or so."

On the TV in the waiting room, CNN was running a live update on the recent foiled terrorist attack on an oil tanker in the Gulf of Mexico. The reporter had the skipper of the Coast Guard vessel that transported Woody, Theo and Waylon next to him. Thag pointed at the television set.

"You boys have been all over the news. It must have been quite a show out there," Thag said.

"It was definitely worth the price of admission," Sheffield said. He watched the news anchor who said that the details of the operation were still sketchy. "That weren't no 'operation.' It was a massacre," Odd said. "And we did the massacring."

Reynolds looked around the waiting room.

"Are Waylon and Maggie in with Woody?" he asked.

"Waylon is back there with him," Thag said. "I guess you haven't heard the news about Maggie."

"What news?" Reynolds asked.

"She's been missing since this morning. They found her Land Cruiser next to your unmarked car this afternoon. Everyone assumed she was with you and Waylon until the Coast Guard reported who was on the boat with you, and the roster did not include her," Thag said.

"They found her car at Point Washington?" Reynolds said.

"Yeah," Thag said.

"Waylon told her to stay at the condo until we contacted her," Shot Glass said. "She must have gotten tired of waiting and followed us to the address where Sheffield, Francis and Woody were hiding out. Have they searched the area?"

"They've been over it with a fine tooth comb. I overheard one of the deputies say that they found footprints they think were hers at the safe house. They led out to some sort of board walk," Thag said.

"If she got there after we left, there wouldn't have been a boat at the slip," Reynolds said.

"There was Captain Woody's old jon boat out there, Detective Reynolds," Sheffield said.

"You don't think she tried to go out on the water in that old thing, do you?" Reynolds was talking to himself out loud.

"She might have thought Woody was still in the vicinity," Odd said.

Reynolds walked over to a phone that hung on the waiting room wall. He dialed zero.

The hospital operator came on the line. "This is official police business. Patch me through to the Walton County sheriff's office," he barked.

He held for a second before he spoke again.

"Dispatch? This is Detective Reynolds. Yeah, that's right Shot Glass. I need to talk to Chief Deputy Arceneau pronto about a missing person named Maggie Wilson. He'll know the case."

He held again while the dispatcher tried to patch him through to the chief. In a second, Shot Glass heard a cell phone ring behind him.

"If you want to talk to me, Reynolds, all you have to do is turn around," the chief said.

Reynolds turned and saw Arceneau behind him. Sheffield was nowhere to be seen. The chief hung up his cell phone and stuck it in his belt holster. Shot Glass didn't waste any time getting to the point.

"Chief, are you following the Maggie Wilson investigation? She's Woody's wife, and she has been missing since this morning," Reynolds said.

"I heard about it. We sent a couple of squad cars out to Point Washington, searched the woods, knocked on some doors. Nobody's seen her."

"I heard you found her footprints on the board walk that leads out to the boat slip," Reynolds said.

Arceneau scratched his head.

"Where do you get this stuff? Are you on my payroll and I just don't know about it?" the chief said.

"I try to keep my ear to the ground, chief. You know, just the way any good law enforcement officer does his job," Reynolds said.

"Yeah, they found footprints that led to the boardwalk. They searched the area around the boat slip and found no signs of foul play. As a matter of fact, they found nothing," the chief said.

"Did you send any boats out on the search?" Reynolds asked.

"I hate to ask this, but why would that have been a good idea?" Arceneau said.

"Because when we left that slip this morning there was a jon boat tied to one of the pilings at the pier. I suspect Maggie may have gotten in that skiff," Reynolds said.

The chief deputy thought about it. "This is the first time I've heard about the jon boat. How big is it?"

From behind them, another voice replied.

"Eight feet. It's green with a flat bow and stern."

It was Waylon. He had come to the waiting room while Woody slept off his anesthesia.

"My mom has rowed that boat a thousand miles in her life. There's no telling where she could be by now," he said to the chief.

"That complicates things, then. Point Washington is near the Canyon. If she got to the bay she could have entered the Intracoastal and gone east towards Panama City, or she could have turned west. If she went west, she could be anywhere between Point Washington and the east pass at Destin harbor.

That's ten miles as the crow flies," Arceneau said. "I'll call in my guys and have them begin to search from Point Washington west. I'll get on the horn and have the Bay County chief handle the eastern section."

"Thanks, chief," Shot Glass said. He meant it.

The chief took Shot Glass' arm and led him aside.

"I came over here tonight to see Theo," he said. "He's going to be fine as far as his wound is concerned. But he's looking at some serious time behind this jail break thing. Do you think Thag might have a trick or two up his sleeve that could help him out?"

Shot Glass looked over at Thag. He was asleep again. He had increased the snoring decibels.

"He doesn't look like much, but he has a lot of fight in him. I'll see what I can do. Theo is a good boy. He deserves a break," Reynolds said.

The chief patted Shot Glass on the arm before he turned and walked out of the waiting room.

Shot Glass looked at Waylon. "If we can find Sheffield, I think the three of us need to get back to the boat."

"He's hiding in the men's room. I'll get my jacket and meet you in the lobby," Waylon said.

AT NINE-THIRTY, THE guardsmen escorted Shot Glass, Waylon and Sheffield to the slip at the Coast Guard station where the Parker boat awaited them. When Shot Glass passed the port side of the bow, he stopped. He reached with his right hand and felt the place on the hull where *Nothing Left to Lose* appeared. He found the seam where tape covered the real name of the boat and peeled it off to reveal the lettering underneath: *Miss Maggie*.

Waylon did the same thing on the starboard side.

Waylon and Shot Glass walked to a trash can the size of an oil drum on the pier and threw the two strips of tape with the faux name of the boat in the trash at the same time.

"Now let's go find Miss Maggie," Shot Glass said as the three men boarded the ship.

Chapter 47

THEY CAME OUT of the Coast Guard station on Alligator Bayou and headed north and west across St. Andrew Bay. They took the Intracoastal and followed it across West Bay to the Canyon.

Sheffield was at the helm, Waylon his first mate.

"Momma would never have tried to row through the Canyon," Waylon said to Shot Glass who stood behind him in the cabin as the *Miss Maggie* cut through the water.

"I don't think so either. Mostly likely she searched for us and when she didn't find us, she let the jon boat drift a while. The current would have taken her towards Destin if she made it into the bay," Shot Glass said.

It was a new moon, a perfect night for a terrorist attack, a terrible one for a search and rescue mission. Shot Glass walked out on the forward section of the boat and turned on the spotlight, swiveled it side to side. The search beam illuminated a thin sliver of water and left a vast universe black and inaccessible. They passed through the Canyon and entered Choctawhatchee Bay near Point Washington. Odd spelled Shot Glass on the spotlight while Waylon took the wheel.

"She could be anywhere out here," Waylon said to Shot Glass.

"We'll find her," Shot Glass said. "Keep close to the southern shore of the bay. Something tells me that's where she'll be," Shot Glass said.

They made their way along the crooked shore line, in and out of bayous, across narrow flats. By one-thirty in the morning they had reached the Highway 331 Bridge that spanned the east section of Choctawhatchee Bay. Along the highway on the east and west sides, granite boulders protected the road from the harsh salt water of the bay that sought to devour any man-made structures. On the east side of the highway an access road trickled down to a public boat ramp.

As they prepared to pass under the bridge, Odd shined the light along the granite monoliths. He caught a glimpse of an object.

"Come around, Waylon," Sheffield said. "I think I saw something." He pointed toward a spot along the west side of the highway.

Waylon maneuvered the *Miss Maggie* until it was offshore ten yards from the object. He dropped anchor.

"It's the jon boat all right," Sheffield said as he shined the bright light on it.

"Momma, Momma," Waylon yelled.

No answer.

He cried out again.

"Is anybody there?"

A weak voice from near the water's edge replied, "Help. I'm here." It was Maggie.

"Take the wheel," Waylon shouted to Sheffield.

Waylon ran to the back of the boat where he knew the water was deep, dived head first into the bay. He swam to the jetty and hurled himself up on the rocks. He got to his feet and hopped from stone to stone until he jumped to the grass near the road.

"Help me," Maggie cried out from the water.

Waylon searched the shoreline until he found her. She was in the cold autumn water from her waist down, her hands holding desperately to a rock that jutted out of the bank.

Waylon sat down on the side of the bank and lowered himself until he was within reach of her.

"We're here, Momma. We're going to get you out," he said to Maggie.

"Hurry, son. I can't last much longer," Maggie said.

Shot Glass and Sheffield watched from the bow of the boat.

"Call for an ambulance. Tell them we're on the road to the boat ramp at the 331 bridge," Waylon shouted.

He reached down with both hands and took Maggie by the wrists. He braced his feet on a granite boulder and pulled back.

Maggie's body slid up the rock surface and he had her on dry land.

He stooped down and lifted her in his arms. She had lost consciousness.

Waylon stood up with Maggie in his arms. He thought for a second how it seemed he carried a small bird, a delicate creature that had not only brought him into the world and nurtured him to manhood, but withstood countless storms that would have laid waste to the entire British fleet. He bowed his head and kissed her on the forehead.

"Hold on, Momma. Help is on the way," he said.

Chapter 48

BARELY FIVE HOURS after the medical team at Gulf Coast Medical Center had treated Maggie for hypothermia and weather exposure and sent her to a room sedated but in stable condition, Waylon and Shot Glass entered the Walton County DA's office with Pythagoras Clemons.

Thag approached the receptionist, Ms. Glasscock. When she looked up at him from reading her Sunday school lesson, she had a look on her face that was blank, but nonetheless severe.

"Can I help you, sir?" she asked.

She took her reading glasses off as if it were an imposition, marked her place in the pamphlet with her right index finger.

"Do you ever watch the national news, Ms. Glasscock?" Thag asked her.

"Of course I do. How may I help you, sir?" She was growing impatient.

"Did you see the story about the men who prevented the terrorist attack on an oil tanker near Panama City yesterday?"

"Everyone has seen it, sir. How may I help you?" She wasn't going to ask him again.

"These are the guys who did that," Thag said as he pointed at Waylon and Shot Glass.

Ms. Glasscock leaned to her right so she could see around Thag. Waylon and Shot Glass smiled at her. The receptionist never changed her expression. She leaned back to her usual position and stared at Thag.

"So?" she said.

"So, these national heroes need a minute with RBJ if he's not too busy," Thag said. "Their names are Waylon Wilson and Shot Glass Reynolds. I'm Thag Clemons, attorney for Woody Wilson, another of the heroes."

"Please sit down over there, and I'll see if Mr. Brightwell can work you in," she said.

"Like hell I will," Thag said. He motioned at Waylon and Shot Glass.

They stood up and walked past the receptionist's desk towards Brightwell's office.

"If you don't stop this minute, I'll call security," the receptionist said.

"Call away," Thag said as he strolled by her.

When they came to Brightwell's office, his door was closed. Thag put his ear to it.

"It sounds like he's on the phone with someone. C'mon," he said to Waylon and Reynolds.

Thag opened the door and walked in to Rudd's office. The district attorney was standing at the window with the phone pressed against his ear. When he saw the three men enter his private domain without invitation, he put his hand over the receiver.

"What the hell, Thag? Get out of here until I finish this call. It's the governor," Brightwell said.

"Fuck you, Rudd," Thag said. He sat down in a chair in front of Rudd's desk and pointed at two other chairs. Waylon and Reynolds took their seats on command.

Brightwell took his hand off the mouthpiece of the phone. "Yes, Governor. I understand the significance of the moment. I won't let you down. Thank you, sir."

Rudd hung up the phone and sat down in his overstuffed chair. He raised his eyebrows.

"I suppose you know who these guys are, Rudd," Thag began.

Rudd looked at the men. "If I am not mistaken, they are Mr. Wilson and Detective Reynolds," he said. "It's a pleasure to see both of you again." His voiced was strained. He looked like he had an olive pit caught in his throat in addition to the usual cob he had up his ass.

Shot Glass and Waylon nodded.

"What can I do for you, Thag?" Brightwell said.

Thag laid it out for him.

"Here's the deal. In about five minutes, we're going to walk out of your office to the courthouse lobby. When we get there, journalists for every major media outlet in this country will ask us for a statement about the fates of three men who face criminal charges in this county: Woody Wilson, Odessa Sheffield and Theophilus Francis.

"Those men distinguished themselves under fire yesterday when they foiled a major terrorist attack on an oil tanker. If that attack had succeeded, your county would be awash in oil this morning, and our country would face one of its greatest defeats.

"We would like to report to those journalists that Rudd Brightwell, Jr., the district attorney of Walton County, is a man who recognizes heroism when he sees it and understands justice and fairness. Such a man would consider the deeds these men performed yesterday as payment in full for any of their former transgressions, if any.

"We would like you to accompany us to the microphone and make the announcement that all charges against these three men have been dismissed with prejudice, that those charges are gone for good."

Rudd squirmed in his chair. His ears were laid back against the sides of his head like a mule's when he would like to kick someone.

"It's funny, Thag. I just heard the same thing from the governor," Brightwell said.

"The governor is a man known to reward his friends and destroy his enemies, Rudd," Thag said.

"I know," Brightwell said.

Thag continued.

"You will also announce the formation of an Alzheimer's task force in Walton County. Its purpose would be to reform the criminal justice system so that people who suffer from Alzheimer's who find themselves ensnared in that system receive prompt treatment from qualified experts in the field. The end result would be to ensure that the system recognizes Alzheimer's for what it is and doesn't turn a blind eye to it. As chairman of that task force, I would work closely with you to confirm that your office complies with the task force's vision. You would report to me quarterly."

Rudd's face grew redder by the minute.

"Finally, you will announce that Woody Wilson is a great patriot, a man who despite the hold the dread disease held on him rallied to fight for his country one last time. You will extend your sincerest apology to him and his family for any harm your uninformed actions may have caused them," Thag said. He stopped and waited for Rudd to speak.

"I think I know the answer to this, but what happens if I refuse to play along with your proposal," Brightwell said. He fidgeted with his Zippo lighter in his left hand.

"Under that scenario, I will tell the media that the district attorney of Walton County should be the subject of a federal investigation. I will call on the Department of Justice to review all your files to determine on how many occasions you have used the brute power of this office to crush those who are least capable of defending themselves, old people with dementia. I would also probably hint that Rudd Brightwell, Jr. is the sort of man who would not hesitate to resort to terrorism himself if it served his own petty political agenda," Thag said.

"Wait a minute," Rudd said. "You know I didn't have any connection to those terrorists. That's preposterous. It's nothing but rank character assassination."

"Sort of like the rank character assassination you were ready to employ toward Woody Wilson, I suppose," Thag said his voice growing softer. "What's good for the goose is good for the gander."

"Anything else?" Rudd asked. He stood clenching and unclenching his fists in suppressed anger.

Thag paused a minute. "Oh, yeah. I almost forgot one thing," he said.

"Let's have it," Brightwell said.

He leaned back in his chair and refused to make eye contact with Waylon and Reynolds.

"You need to fire that bitch at the front desk," Thag said.

Waylon couldn't stifle a snicker when he heard the last condition. It was the first he knew of it.

Rudd stood up and tightened his tie. He went to the hall tree and took down his jacket, slipped his arms through the sleeves. He shook hands with the three men.

"Let's not keep the press waiting, gentlemen," he said as he walked out the door ahead of them.

Before Thag could leave Brightwell's office, Shot Glass caught him by the sleeve. He handed him a business card. On the back he had written a name and phone number.

"This is the contact information for my captain in Nashville," he said. "Would you mind calling him and delivering a speech along the lines of the one you just gave Rudd?"

Thag slapped him on the back and stuck the card in his pocket. "It would be my pleasure, Detective Reynolds," he said.

Waylon, Shot Glass and Thag filed out of Rudd's office and walked down the hallway to the lobby. They could see Rudd ahead of them as he stopped at the front desk and said something to Ms. Glasscock. She looked at Brightwell like he had come at her with a butcher knife, laid her hands flat on her desk for a second, then opened a drawer, removed her purse and stood up to leave.

Thag shot her the finger on his way out the door.

Chapter 49

AFTER THE PRESS conference, Shot Glass and Waylon parted ways with Thag and left to deliver the news to Woody and Maggie, the news that they would be free to live the rest of their lives together, free from false accusations and prison shackles, fettered only by Alzheimer's.

They swung by the new Northwest Florida Beaches International Airport on the west side of the bay near Panama City to pick up Jessie. They waited for her in baggage claim. "I guess our adventure is almost over, Shot Glass. It's been a helluva ride," Waylon said.

"It has indeed," Reynolds said.

Waylon felt a tug on the back of his shirt.

"Can you guys direct me to the elite special forces unit for Homeland Security?" a voice said.

Waylon turned around and saw Jessie. She had her spend-the-night at the hospital clothes on, a loose-fitting Robin's egg blue Seagrove Beach sweat shirt, white shorts, pink ASICS running shoes. She had her hair pulled up in a ponytail and wore no makeup.

"The most heroic thing I did was manage not to soil my pants," he said to her. He hugged her with both arms, lifted her feet off the floor.

"Shot Glass was 'the man' out there," Waylon said.

Jessie gave Reynolds a hug, too.

"Thanks for bringing Woody and Maggie home to us safe and sound," she said.

"They're the finest people I know. I'm glad everything worked out like it did," Shot Glass said.

Waylon grabbed Jessie's bag from the conveyor. It was large enough to supply American forces in Afghanistan for at least two weeks. He extended the suit case handle and rolled the bag behind him as they walked to the car.

"I'll drive if you love birds want to get in the back seat," Shot Glass said when they reached Waylon's 4 Runner. Waylon tossed him the keys and got in the back seat with Jessie. They cuddled up next to each other.

As they rode to the hospital, Waylon told Jessie about the press conference.

"What's the latest news on Maggie and Woody?" she asked.

"We left the hospital about three thirty this morning," Waylon said. "The doctors said they would have daddy in an induced coma until this afternoon to give him a chance to rest. Momma's vital signs all looked good. She was dehydrated and sunburned, had some scratches from her fall on the rocks, but no broken bones or other serious injuries. They knocked her out with sedatives, too, and put her in a private room. She should be ready to receive guests by the time we get there."

Jessie patted Waylon on his leg. "I can't wait to see Maggie's face when you tell her about the DA. It will be a dream come true for her," she said.

"For all of us," Waylon said.

When they arrived at the hospital, they boarded the elevator, and rode to the floor where Maggie had a private room.

They stepped off the elevator and the charge nurse saw them.

She motioned for Waylon.

"Your mom woke up about an hour and half ago. She insisted that we take her to see Mr. Wilson," she said. She looked away from Waylon when she spoke. He sensed that something was up.

"Momma can be insistent," Waylon said. "Where is she now?"

"We rolled her bed down to surgical ICU. She's with your dad," the charge nurse said. The other nurses at the nurses' station had busied themselves looking at patients' charts while their supervisor gave Waylon the report.

"It's okay. She's been missing him something awful the last few weeks. You did the right thing," Waylon said.

"I hope so," the charge nurse said.

Jessie, Waylon and Shot Glass rode the elevator to the second floor and got off at SICU. The charge nurse had called ahead. The director of nurses met them when they stepped off the elevator. "Mr. Wilson?" she said. She hadn't met him before.

"I'm Mr. Wilson," Waylon said.

"When they brought your mom down from her room, we rolled her next to Mr. Wilson so she could see he was all right. When she saw him, she calmed down and drifted back to sleep. We checked on both of them every fifteen minutes and they were doing fine, resting peacefully," she said.

"Yes, ma'am," Waylon said. He waited for the other shoe to drop.

"About ten minutes ago, one of the nurses checked on them again, right on schedule," she said.

Jessie put her left arm around Waylon's waist. Shot Glass stood behind them. They knew there was no need for further explanations.

"Come with me," the director of nurses said. "We knew you were on your way, so we left them alone."

Surgical ICU was one large room. The patient census was low, so it was quiet save for the hum of monitoring equipment.

There were no private cubicles. Dark gray curtains hung from ceiling racks to provide patients some semblance of privacy.

The director of nurses walked ahead of them down the middle of the room. On their left, they passed a man in his fifties, his leg wrapped in bandages after a knee replacement.

On the right, they saw a woman in her thirties, her left wrist in a splint from an injury she received when she stubbed her toe on an uneven place in the sidewalk as she jogged near her home.

The nurse supervisor walked towards the far wall until she reached the curtain that created the last patient stall. She stopped and waited for Waylon, Shot Glass and Jessie to catch up. When they came next to her, she turned to Waylon.

"Take as much time as you need," she said. She turned and they watched her as she walked back to the nurses' station, sat down and put her face in her hands. She didn't look back at them.

Waylon and Jessie held hands.

Waylon looked at Shot Glass. He could tell Reynolds felt like an intruder. "It's all right, Detective Reynolds," he said. "We want you to be here with us."

Jessie nodded at Shot Glass.

They took a couple of steps forward so they could see around the curtain.

They saw two hospital beds. Maggie had lowered the rail on the left side of her bed, the right side of Woody's. She had taken the IVs out of their arms, and a slight trickle of blood seeped from each wound. She had left her bed and joined Woody in his.

She was curled up against Woody. He had wrapped the fingers of his left hand around her right hand, placed it on his chest. The corners of his mouth were turned up to form the biggest grin of his life. Maggie's lips were next to Woody's cheek, pursed in a kiss.

Waylon moved close to his parents, reached out and touched their cold bodies. He put his arms around both of them at the same time, hugged them and began to cry. As he sobbed, Jessie came next to him. She rubbed his back with her left hand, reached out her right and brushed a strand of hair away from Maggie's face.

Shot Glass took a handkerchief from his pants pocket and wiped tears that ran down his face.

He took a few steps, stood with his back to the wall.

"Though rosy lips and cheeks within his bending sickle's

compass come," he said softly and closed his eyes while Waylon and Jessie grieved.

Chapter 50

SHOT GLASS ROSE before daybreak and put on his funeral clothes, a pair of khaki pants, brown Justin roper boots, a starched white long-sleeved cotton shirt, a navy windbreaker with "Nashville PD" stenciled in block yellow letters on the back.

He slung his holster around his shoulders and stuck the Kimber .45 he had loaned to Woody Wilson three days earlier in it.

He planned to return to Nashville that evening after the service, so he packed his clothes and toiletries and checked his briefcase. He threw his room key on the bed, grabbed his things, walked out the door and checked the lock to be sure it fastened behind him.

He wasn't hungry, but it didn't matter. He stopped by the Donut Hole for breakfast.

When the doors of Ocean Bank in Seagrove Beach opened for business at nine o'clock, he went in and asked to see the president.

"Tell him Linus Schmutzer sent me," he told the lady at the front desk.

In a minute, a fat bald man in a gray three-piece suit came out of a corner office and approached him.

"Detective Reynolds, I'm Bill Martin, president of Ocean Bank," he said. He talked like a man who was sorry to disturb people with his opinions. Shot Glass hadn't said anything to the receptionist about being a detective.

They shook hands and Martin invited Shot Glass into his office.

"What can I do for you, today, Detective Reynolds?" Martin asked.

Shot Glass took the pendant key ring with the "HS" symbol on it and laid it on Martin's desk.

"I need to pick up whatever it is that this key gives me access to. Linus Schmutzer told me he had already given you instructions about it," Reynolds said.

"Mr. Schmutzer told me to expect you," Martin said. "Please follow me."

Reynolds figured that Martin was not the sort of a man who made small talk, especially with detectives. He trailed behind Martin to the vault where the bank kept its safe deposit boxes.

Martin inserted the key into box nineteen, withdrew a drawer and placed it on a table in the middle of the room.

"Let the guard know when you're through, and he will call me," Martin said. He pointed at a large black man in a security guard uniform that stood at the vault entrance.

"Will do, President Martin," Shot Glass said.

When Reynolds was alone in the vault, he looked in the drawer. It contained one white envelope. Reynolds removed the envelope and turned it over. Someone had written Reynolds' name on the front of the envelope, sealed the back with invisible tape.

Shot Glass stuck the envelope in the inside pocket of his windbreaker, slid the safe deposit drawer back into the wall, locked it and removed the key. He nodded at the security guard as he walked out of the vault. He walked through the bank lobby, out the front door, got in his cruiser and set course for the Methodist church in Point Washington.

Chapter 51

AT TWO O'CLOCK a small group of people assembled in Point Washington around the Gilbert family plot in the cemetery a stone's throw from the waters of the bay.

Waylon asked the Methodist preacher to keep it simple. "My folks weren't much for pomp and circumstance," he said.

Shot Glass, Thag, Odessa Sheffield and Theophilus Francis stood off to the side while the pastor read a few passages of scripture, prayed too long a prayer. Theo had his arm in a sling.

Hank Cumberland had already set the double headstone. Above Woody's name he chiseled the words from the note Maggie left him, "He never forgot how much he loved us." Maggie had not given him any instructions about her own inscription, so he chose words from one of Shakespeare's sonnets, "Love's not Time's Fool".

After the benediction, the preacher shook hands with the family members and left. People milled around the graves for a few minutes before they returned to their cars and went back to their regular lives.

Waylon, Jessie and their two daughters lingered by the tombstone for a few minutes. Shot Glass walked Thag, Odd and Theo to the parking lot. Theo had tears in his eyes. "I wish I had more time with Captain Woody," he said.

Sheffield put his arm around Theo's shoulder.

"We all do, son," he said. "All we can do now is live the way Woody would have wanted us to live."

"Amen," Shot Glass said.

Thag nodded at the men.

Reynolds sat in his cruiser and watched as Theo, Odd and Thag drove out of the parking lot. In a few minutes, Waylon and Jessie stopped by his car. Waylon rapped his knuckles against the driver's side window, and Shot Glass rolled down the window.

"Drop by the condo for a few minutes before you leave town," he said.

Shot Glass nodded at him and rolled the window up as Waylon walked away.

When everyone had left, Reynolds got out of his car and walked back into the cemetery. At the gravesite he saw an old man with a long white beard. He had a cane in his right hand and leaned on it while he looked at the headstone, his head bowed.

Reynolds stood at the foot of the grave for a few minutes before he approached the old man. "Still a master of disguise, I see, Linus," he said.

"It's hard to teach an old dog new tricks, Detective Reynolds," Schmutzer said. He was still looking at the headstone.

Shot Glass pulled the envelope from the safe deposit box out of his pocket. He had broken the seal and read the contents.

Schmutzer looked at the envelope in Reynolds' hand.

"Now that you have read my letter, I hope you understand I am not altogether the monster you believed me to be," Schmutzer began.

"The medical establishment in this country, blinded by its insatiable greed, cares more about face lifts and boob jobs than it does about people like Woody Wilson, people who wage losing battles for years against Alzheimer's disease. Perhaps my methods were diabolical at times, but unlike my Uncle Linus, I acted not out of cruelty. Rather, I searched for a cure," Schmutzer said.

"Did you find one?" Reynolds asked.

"Had I found one, I would have cured Woody," Schmutzer said. He glanced at the headstone.

"At least you tried, Doc Smooth," Reynolds said. He extended his hand to Schmutzer.

Schmutzer shook Reynolds' hand.

Before he released his grip, Shot Glass looked Schmutzer in the eye. "If I ever see you again, Linus, I'll arrest you for the murder of Dr. Richard Davis," he said.

Shot Glass turned and walked to his car. He started the engine, put the vehicle in drive and idled out of the parking lot.

When he came to the road, he turned towards Seagrove Beach. As he passed the cemetery, he looked to the left to catch one last glimpse of the final resting places of Woody and Maggie Wilson.

Linus Schmutzer was gone.

THE END

Stephen Woodfin practices law and writes books in Kilgore, Texas.

Please visit his Amazon Author Page to find a complete listing of his books.

If you follow Stephen on Twitter @stephenwoodfin, he will follow you back.

He blogs regularly at http://venturegalleries.com/author/stephenwoodfin, so please drop by and join the conversation.

www.ingramcontent.com/pod-product-compliance
Lightning Source LLC
Chambersburg PA
CBHW060530260626
47161CB00003B/839